321- 1470

Lancaster County Second Chances 3

RUTH PRICE

ISBN: **1515244326**
ISBN-13: **978-1515244325**

TABLE OF CONTENTS

ACKNOWLEDGMENTS

All Praise first to the Almighty God who has given me this wonderful opportunity to share my words and stories with the world. Next, I have to thank my family, especially my husband Harold who supports me even when I am being extremely crabby. Further, I have to thank my wonderful friends and associates with Global Grafx Press who support me in every way as a writer. Lastly, I wouldn't be able to do any of this without you, my readers. I hold you in my heart and prayers and hope that you enjoy my books.

All the best and Blessings,
Ruth.

CHAPTER ONE

Singing. Cora Lapp closed her eyes and drank in the sound. The women's high, ethereal voices were reaching to the sky. The men sang in reply, their deep booming voices adding depth and earthiness, adding that rich weight, that groundedness. Singing had always been Cora's favorite part of Amish worship, even when she didn't feel the emotions that she guessed she was supposed to feel in church.

As far she was concerned, the service was over when the singing was over. She had never gotten much from the sermons. They went *on and on* until the elderly and children were nodding towards sleep, and even the adults were stupefied with boredom. Why did everyone have to make such a big deal about it? Wasn't *singing* worship enough?

Not that she had a lot of experience with worship. In spite of her Amish upbringing, she had never had much of an impulse toward God. She believed in God, but mostly she thought of Him as someone who disliked fun things.

And the people who wanted them.

When she thought of God, it was with the uncomfortable certainty that He was probably mad at her. Or at least, that scenario would make the most sense: she had almost none of the restraint that a good Amish person was supposed to have. She loved feeling pretty, she loved stylish clothes and makeup, she wanted to have fun, and the thought of spending the rest of her life in one place, reading the *Bible*, made her feel as if the walls were closing in.

The singing swelled again. One corner of Cora's lip curled up in the whisper of a smile. Now she could detect Isaac Muller's voice. Poor Isaac, he was an enthusiastic singer, he sang with all his heart, but he was *always* off key, and when the spirit really moved him, he sang *loudly*.

She opened her eyes just a crack. The worship service was being held in Jabez Stoltzfus' barn and there had been too many people for all of them to fit inside. Isaac had been late that morning and had to take a seat in one of the folding chairs set up in the yard outside. Even so, *no one* could miss him.

Cora watched him through her lashes. The morning sun crowned his white-blonde hair with light, glanced off the strong planes of his face, touched his lips with a shining finger. Looking at him now, she was amazed that she had never before appreciated how handsome her childhood playmate had become.

Because he was *very* handsome. He was six feet tall, his shoulders were like a two-by-four, he was almost all muscle, and his eyes were as big and blue and soulful as a baby's. Maybe it had just taken awhile for her to see the adult Isaac, rather than her childhood neighbor.

But as Isaac sang in the springtime sunshine, Cora could safely say that she was seeing him *now*. In fact, she felt a strong desire to see more of him, and more clearly, than ever before. She let her gaze drift down past his shoulders, and wondered what Isaac looked like without his clothes.

The thought jolted her back to the present. She shifted her weight uncomfortably and fanned herself with one hand. Yes, it was safe to say that she was *not* a good Amish person. God was probably thinking about *smiting* her at that very moment.

The singing ended, and Brother Johanssen stood up to expound. They were in for it now, and for a good two hours. Cora sighed and closed her eyes again.

***

After what seemed like forever to Cora, the sermon finally ended. After the sermon (which, to Cora's annoyance, took *exactly* two hours), the meeting slowly broke up and everyone gathered for a lunch on the grounds.

Like most of the other women, Cora helped to serve the men at lunch. It was a good opportunity for her to get close to Isaac, and she seized the chance. She had a jug of tea, and worked toward him while trying not to look *too* obvious. She couldn't honestly say that she cared much about Amish rules -- she thought most were silly -- but *Isaac* cared, and for his sake she was trying to conform.

At least *outwardly*.

To Cora's annoyance, the way to Isaac was temporarily blocked by another girl. Leah Hauser was serving Isaac some kind of bread, and Cora turned to serve a few of the other men while she waited. When she turned back again, Leah was still there, talking to Isaac and – yes, tossing her head and laughing. Leah was a pretty brunette with big brown eyes. If she had tried to flirt with Isaac even six months earlier, Cora might have been alarmed. But at this point in their relationship, she was certain enough of Isaac not to feel threatened.

But *still*.

Cora sighed and resisted the impulse to roll her eyes. She let a few more moments pass, and when Leah didn't take herself off voluntarily, she sidled over and leaned across Leah to pour Isaac a glass of tea.

"Excuse me," she smiled, with as fair an approximation of innocence as she could muster. "Oh, Leah, Carl Johansen asked me to tell you that he wanted some of that bread, if you don't mind."

Leah's eyes held skepticism, but Cora had left her no graceful way to refuse. "Of course," she murmured, and withdrew reluctantly.

Cora watched her go, undecided whether to feel annoyance or amusement. But in any case, Leah wouldn't be coming back right away. Carl Johansen was sitting at a table clear across the yard. By the time Leah realized her little trick, she'd have had at least a few minutes to talk to Isaac.

"How does that tea taste, Isaac?" she asked sweetly. "Too dry? Shall I add a little *sugar*?"

Isaac was so transparently pleased by her attention that Cora had a hard time suppressing a smile. He was still nearly as sweet and guileless as he had been as a child.

She found it close to *irresistible*.

"Ummm… let me see." Isaac lifted the glass to his lips with an exaggerated expression of fine deliberation. "You know, I think it *is* too dry."

"Oh, that won't do. Let me bring you another glass." She leaned across him again, this time so close that her breath grazed across his ear. To her gratification, when she stood back, Isaac was looking more pleased than ever, and his cheeks were beet red.

Cora pursed her lips, well pleased – but as she turned, she caught Johan Eckhard's eye. He was sitting at the same table, had noticed everything, and he was barely stifling an amused comment. His wife, Berta, was wearing a less charitable expression.

Cora straightened, swallowing her laughter. For Isaac's sake, she really *should* behave. But it really was kind of fun to ruffle a few feathers.

It was so pitifully *easy*.

She scanned the crowd for her rival, estimating how long she'd be gone. To Cora's amusement, Leah was now completely bogged down with Carl Johanssen, who really *did* seem to have a lot of additional requests.

But, better safe than sorry.

So she stepped out of sight of Isaac's table, just long enough to put her pitcher down, scribble a few lines on a small napkin, and turn right back around.

She sidled up to Isaac. "Here you go," she purred, leaning in close as she poured.

"That was fast," Berta Eckhard drawled.

Cora shot the woman her sunniest smile. "I try to be useful," she replied, and while she was pouring with one hand, her other hand quietly dropped the scrap of paper onto Isaac's lap, where he quickly covered it with his hand.

It was the system they'd been using for months now. So far, it seemed to be working.

"Now, how do you like that?" she beamed.

"Oh, that's *great*," Isaac smiled.

She dared to give him the tiniest, the most furtive of winks, but she was leaving, she heard Johan Eckhard snort with inappropriate laughter.

As she walked back to the house, Cora couldn't help thinking that her tiny intrigue with Isaac was probably the most interesting thing he'd seen happen at church that day.

***

When her pitcher was empty, Cora made her way back into the Stoltzfus house. It was as busy as a hive of bees, with dozens of women buzzing back and forth from the kitchen. There, the queen bee, Fannie Stoltzfus, was the calm center at this storm of activity. Fannie was a husky, middle-aged woman, almost man-tall. She wore her brown hair in thick braids on top of her head, and wore tiny round glasses. She was the local schoolteacher, and was therefore an excellent manager.

"Elena, here's the soufflé. Mary, I need more forks. Kirsten, can you start another pot of coffee? Thank you."

Only a few people could stand in the kitchen at one time, and girls were waiting at the kitchen doorway three or four deep. Cora stood patiently, waiting her turn in line.

As she waited, Cora slowly began to notice that the other

girls in line were talking to each other -- but not to her. Sometimes, they whispered.

And laughed. Occasionally, Cora thought she heard her own name.

Her chance to see Isaac, even briefly, had put her into a good mood, but that good feeling was fading fast. She felt the skin on the back of her neck tingling. She'd *like* to believe the other girls weren't talking about her, but since this kind of thing happened every time she went out in public, the odds of that were pretty slim. She didn't know for sure how much of her story the other girls had heard, but in a community as small as theirs, it was safe to assume that by now, they knew *everything* about her disastrous rumspringa.

Cora folded her arms across her chest and tossed her head. Even her old school friends had become cold and distant, and Cora had the growing sense that the women in the community, and especially the younger women, didn't like her.

At *all*.

Cora bit her lip angrily. This cold reception was one of the reasons she couldn't imagine herself joining the church. How could she ever make a life here when most of the girls her own age hated her? And their hate was so baseless, so *stupid*. It wasn't like she was chasing *their* boyfriends, or flirting with every man in town. She'd never looked twice at anyone but Isaac. And if they didn't like her relationship with *him* --

well, that was just too bad.

A soft tug at Cora's sleeve interrupted her angry thoughts. When she turned, Leah Hauser was standing there, payback sparkling in her brown eyes. She shoved an empty tray into Cora's hands.

"Oh, Cora, Carl Johanssen says he's out of bread. Could you be a dear and get some for him? I'll take the pitcher. I'm sure Isaac Muller's out of tea by now."

Leah half-turned to enjoy the tinkling laughter of the other girls. Then her eyes returned to Cora's.

"Don't want to miss an opportunity to circulate, eh Cora?" she smiled.

Cora's blue eyes narrowed. She was pulling her arm back to *slap the snot* out of Leah Hauser when the laughter abruptly died. Cora felt, rather than saw, Fannie Stoltzfus' shadow. An arm went around her shoulders, and she froze.

"Oh, Cora, I'm so glad you're here. I could use another pair of hands right now, and you're always so clever. Come and help me."

Cora allowed herself to be dragged away, but she was intensely conscious of the eyes on her back. She wondered vaguely why Fannie Stoltzfus had bothered to rescue her, or if the older woman simply hadn't known what was going on. One thing was for sure, though: if Fannie Stoltzfus hadn't shown up when she did, Cora was sure she would've slapped

Leah Hauser blind. And that her last chance of living down her rumspringa would've vanished.

So she stood by Fannie Stoltzfus for the next hour, passing plates and dishes and utensils to the women who were lining up for them. Cora kept her eyes on her hands. She was afraid that if she lifted them, everyone would see that her anger had already faded, and that she was dangerously close to tears.

When the busiest part of lunch had passed, Fannie Stoltzfus took Cora's hand and whispered, "Come with me. I want to talk to you."

She led Cora out of the kitchen the back way, to a narrow stairway that led up to the second floor. Mrs. Stoltzfus opened the door to a small, sparsely furnished room with a few chairs and a table.

She closed the door and gestured to one of the chairs. "Sit down, Cora. I'd like to talk to you."

Cora braced herself for a lecture. Mrs. Stoltzfus had noticed after all. She was going to be called out for almost slapping Leah. Or possibly, for corrupting Isaac with her wicked tea-pouring skills.

So she was surprised when instead, Fannie Stoltzfus said, "Your mother tells me that you're looking for a job, Cora. Would you be open to doing something around here?"

Cora stared at the older woman. *Was she joking?* How could this conversation *not* be about the brawl that had almost happened downstairs?

"Um… yes. Yes, I am looking for something to do," she replied tentatively.

"Good. I'm looking for some help at school. Just between us, I'm going to take some time off of teaching, and I'll need someone to take over while I'm gone. My daughter Mary is a wonderful apprentice, but I think the children would benefit from two teachers. It's hard for one person to look after everything."

Cora blinked, nonplussed. She had never even *imagined* herself as a teacher. She hadn't disliked school as a child, but she'd spent most of her time giggling and whispering to her classmates.

"I… I don't have any experience doing that," she replied. "I'm not a…" she quickly caught herself before blurting, *nerd*. She carefully amended, "…*teacher type*."

Mrs. Stoltzfus nodded. "No, but I need the help, and you need the job. I think you'd make a fine apprentice teacher, but of course it's up to you. Think about it. I'll need to know fairly soon, though."

She rose and put her hand on the doorknob. Just before she turned it, she looked back over her shoulder and added archly -- "And for the love of Heaven, Cora, *stop teasing Leah Hauser.*

"She's jealous enough already."

CHAPTER TWO

"It's beautiful out tonight."

Katie Lapp sat at a dresser in front of her bedroom window, brushing her long brown hair. Joseph, her husband, was splayed out on their bed with his eyes closed and his hands pressed to his face. His only response was an exhausted groan.

Katie turned her head to look at him. "You only have yourself to blame," she smiled. "You know better than to work like you're still seventeen."

She set the brush down on her dresser and joined her husband in bed, snuggling up to him. "Joseph, let's go and sit in the swing on the front porch," she whispered. "The children are all in bed, and the stars are out by now. It's so warm out tonight. Remember how much fun we had in my parents' swing, when you were courting with me?"

"We could have been banned," he agreed, without

removing his hands from his face.

"*Mmm*, I remember," she whispered, and tried to nibble on his ear, but he turned his head away.

"Don't tease me tonight, woman," he groaned, "I'm a dead man. A dead man who has to get up before dawn tomorrow."

Katie pulled her mouth down into a pout. "Well! If Joseph Lapp won't kiss me, I guess he *must* be dead," she agreed. She pulled the bed sheets up over his face, giggling. "He was on fire at first, but I guess he's fizzled out now."

"Leave me in peace," he pleaded.

"You're surely not that feeble yet," she wheedled. "Just one kiss? A little one, such a *leeetle* one?"

"Oh, you will be the death of me," he complained, but soon the bed sheet began to move this way and that. Katie was pulled underneath, and disappeared. This was followed by rumbling laughter and delighted squeals, and what sounded unmistakably like loud, slobbery kissing.

"Happy now?"

"Ew, Joseph!"

This was followed by the sound of more conventional kissing for some little while, followed by silence. The sheet moved a little then was still.

"*Joseph?*" Katie whispered. "*I want a baby.*"

"The truth comes out," he sighed. "So you only want me for a baby?" The sheet wiggled again, and Katie laughed.

"Joseph, I mean it."

Joseph's muscular arm rose and flipped the sheet down. Katie was nestled on his chest. He looked down at her.

"You haven't given me much time to think about it," he remarked mildly.

"What *do* you think?" she whispered, her eyes on his.

He ran one large brown hand through his rumpled blonde hair. "I hadn't considered it much. What with everything that's happened with Cora."

"Yes. A lot has happened in a short time. We haven't had much time to ourselves," Katie reminded him.

Joseph looked down at her. "I know. I'm sorry. It hasn't been fair to you."

"I'm not complaining," Katie replied softly. "I would do it all the same. And I know it's been hard on you."

Joseph sighed. "Cora is spoiled, and she can be wild. But she's always been my favorite."

Katie put a hand up to his cheek, caressed it. "Maybe we should invite her back for a week or two. Would you like that?"

He took her hand. "Yes, I would."

"Then it's settled. But if we do that, we won't have this much privacy again in a while. If we're going to have children together, we should *start*. Don't you think?"

Joseph's eyebrows went up. "*Children*? How many do you want?"

"Just one -- at first." Katie's lips curled up mischievously. "But we're running behind."

"Oh, well then," Joseph retorted, and took his giggling wife into his arms.

***

The next morning, the startled Lapp children found themselves alone in the kitchen at daybreak. It was a thing that had never happened before.

Hezekiah looked up toward the stairs, frowning. "Do you think something's wrong?" he asked.

"No Hezekiah," Emma replied in exasperation, as she broke a couple of eggs into a frying pan. "They'll be down in a few minutes."

Hezekiah watched the stairs, unconvinced. "Daed *never* oversleeps," he grumbled.

"Well, *now* he does," Emma told him. "And everybody goes off schedule now and then."

"Everybody who gets *married* you mean," he replied.

"When *I* get a wife, I'm not going to let her interfere with my work."

Emma put a hand to her mouth and began giggling. "That's because you don't know anything about women!" she retorted.

Hezekiah's face went red. His voice was beginning to go squeaky, and he knew that he couldn't shout without making everyone laugh, so he picked up a table napkin and threw it at his sister.

Joseph descended the stairs into the kitchen, pulling on his suspenders. "Here now, that's no way to start the morning," he objected. "What's going on?"

"Hezekiah was *worried* about you," Emma giggled.

"Well, maybe he should be," Joseph deadpanned, winking over his shoulder at Katie. "I'm beginning to feel *unsafe*. I'm like a little deer in the forest. I mind my own business, but there's a big cat in the bushes, waiting to pounce."

"What's *pounce*?" Caleb asked innocently, his blue eyes wide.

Katie went red to the ears and Joseph looked down and rubbed his mouth with his hand.

"You're going to school now, Caleb," he replied, his voice unsteady. "What do cats *usually* do to other animals?"

Caleb perked up. "They *hunt* them!" he proclaimed

triumphantly.

"That's right, my boy. They hide, and crouch down low, and watch for an opportunity. When the prey gets close..."

Katie had an apron in her hands, but at this, she balled it up and threw it at Joseph's head. "I suppose I *caught* you!" she exclaimed, hands on hips. "Joseph Lapp, you should be ashamed. In front of the children, too!"

Joseph pulled the apron off his head and tossed it back. "Large cats have quick tempers, as well, and sometimes attack *even their mates* unpredictably."

"Not so unpredictably!" Katie retorted, tying the apron around her waist.

Joseph threw his head back and laughed, and the sound filled the room. The children joined in, and soon even Katie couldn't resist.

But that didn't keep Hezekiah from whispering to Jeremy: "They're *so* weird. On second thought, I don't think I'm going to get married. *Ever.*"

Jeremy nodded, and the two of them stared at their father, as if appraising his mental health. Their eyes expressed pessimism, and to a lesser extent, scientific curiosity.

Joseph took the cup of coffee that Katie offered to him and put it to his lips. "What would you children think of Aunt Cora coming out to visit us again?" he asked.

Caleb rested his head on his elbows and smiled. "I'd like that," he said. "I like Aunt Cora. She's *fun*."

Emma looked thoughtful. "As long as she doesn't stay in my room," she replied finally.

"She won't," Katie reassured her.

"Boys, what about you?" Joseph asked.

Jeremiah shrugged, and Hezekiah frowned.

"Problem?" Joseph probed.

Hezekiah frowned again and bit his lip, as if deliberating. Finally he blurted: "Some of the girls in town are talking about Aunt Cora," he said finally. "They're saying…"

Joseph cut him short. "I know what they're saying," he replied quietly, "and there's no truth in it. There'll be no talk of that kind in *this* house, young man. Do you understand me?"

Hezekiah nodded and was silent.

"Well, that settles it then," Joseph said briskly. "We'll ask Aunt Cora over to stay with us for a few weeks."

He smiled and slapped his hand on the table, but he and Katie exchanged a long, telling look as she came to the table to serve the bacon.

***

That evening the two of them rocked quietly in the front porch swing. The first blush of summer was in the air; the breeze was cool, but it smelled of freshly turned earth. Joseph put his arm around Katie, and she nestled on his chest.

"I'm glad Cora is coming out to visit us, Joseph. I'm worried about her," Katie confided softly. "I know that she means well, but she's very young, and I don't think she fully understands how other people might interpret her actions."

"How *some* people might interpret her actions," Joseph replied, with a frown. "I agree that she's careless, but I think she's all right, now that she's interested in Isaac Muller. In fact, I can't think of anyone I'd *rather* be with her than Isaac."

"Isaac is with her more than you think," Katie replied in a low voice. "Jeremy told me today that last Sunday he saw Cora pass Isaac a note during worship. Joseph, they're meeting each other in secret."

Joseph sat up suddenly. "What?"

"Why else would they be passing notes? They're meeting somewhere, I tell you. And if word of it gets around, Cora's in trouble."

"Isaac wouldn't do that," Joseph replied, but there was uncertainty in his voice.

"Isaac is head over ears in love with Cora," Katie replied. "Can you see him refusing her, if she asked? He'd do *anything* for her."

"Well, if that's true, why wouldn't he just ask to court with her, in the daylight, like an honest man?" Joseph asked.

Katie frowned. "Be fair, Joseph. It's *Isaac*. You know he wants to ask. He may have asked already." She clasped his hand gently. "No, this has to be Cora. She's still trying to decide who she wants to be. She hasn't figured that out, not yet. So for now, she's got poor Isaac dangling on a string."

"I hope you're wrong," Joseph said at last.

"I hope so, too," Katie agreed. "But all the more reason to invite Cora to stay here with us. We live right next door to the Mullers. If Cora and Isaac are slipping away together, the two of them can at least meet here without the risk of scandal."

Joseph shook his head in frustration. "But what happens when she goes home again? I swear, Kate, sometimes I get so angry that -- that I wish I wasn't Amish – so I could curse!"

Katie looked at him in bemusement, and then burst out laughing.

"I'm glad you *are* Amish," she confided. "And even though you act like it, I'm glad you're not Cora's father. You're not responsible for her."

"Thank God for that," Joseph agreed, sighing.

"Your problem is that you're such a good *daed* you don't know when to quit," Katie told him indulgently.

"My own children haven't given me half the problems," he agreed. "Tell me about *them* for awhile."

Katie nodded. "All right then. Here's som*e easier* news.

"Hezekiah is going to need The Talk soon," she reminded him. "His voice is breaking every other word. And Jeremy is making google eyes at the little redheaded Baum girl. I think her name is Kirsten.

"Oh, and I think Emma had a little bit of a crush on Isaac, for awhile, but I'm pretty sure she's over it now."

Joseph groaned. "Oh, no more news of the lovelorn, not tonight," he begged. "I'll dream all night of Jeremy running away with the redhead, and Emma pining for Isaac."

Katie laughed and kissed him, then added:

"That leaves only Caleb. You'll be glad to know *he* isn't in love with anyone. He came home today and talked for hours about what he learned in school."

She sighed. "But I still can't believe he's even old enough to be in school. I feel like I'm *losing* him," Katie said softly. "He's not a baby anymore."

Joseph looked down at her. "He was already *five* when you first met him," he said lightly, hugging her.

Katie turned her face into his chest. "Don't make fun of me Joseph," she pleaded. "I love him, I can't help it. I want to hang onto him."

"I know," Joseph whispered, and kissed her ear. "But you're going to have to learn how to let go just a little bit."

When he saw that this suggestion met with no enthusiasm, he added lightly: "Maybe you'll settle for holding onto *me?*"

For answer, Katie looked up and twined her arms around him. They stayed there long into the night, until the moon rode high in the sky and the stars fell down onto the fragrant fields.

Dollar play wig cards

Store

bag for vacation

bag zipper bag

Big 3 pin book

acorish book

kitty

CHAPTER THREE

"Aunt Cora!"

Caleb jumped off the front porch and ran toward Cora, who had just climbed down from Isaac Muller's buggy. Cora knelt down to take him into her arms and swing him around in a circle. "Ow! You're getting too big for me now!" she complained.

Katie had just opened the screen door. A shadow fell over her face, but she quickly recovered.

"We're so glad you decided to come visit us, Cora. We've missed you!"

Katie hugged Cora, thinking that the young woman was more beautiful than ever. Cora was wearing little makeup, but her skin glowed pink and her bright eyes sparkled. She was faintly fragrant of tangerines, and she looked so vibrantly happy that Katie began to wonder if she should, in fact, be alarmed.

"Isaac saw me walking over and offered me a ride," Cora explained, smiling back at Isaac.

Katie gave Isaac a searching glance. Their strapping, handsome neighbor looked far too happy for her peace of mind. "Hello, Isaac," she smiled. "It was kind of you to offer Cora a lift. Won't you come in, have dinner with us?"

Isaac smiled and shook his head. "Oh, no, thank you. I have to be going. And I've already had a snack." As evidence, he picked up a half-eaten tangerine.

Katie looked at Cora again, and thought many things.

But what she said was: "Give your parents our love, Isaac! And don't be a stranger. Come by the house sometime."

Isaac seemed almost embarrassed by her kindness. He looked down, and his cheeks went red. "Thank you," he mumbled. His voice sounded subdued -- to Katie's quick ear, troubled.

Then: "Goodbye, Cora." His eyes lingered on Cora's in parting, and Katie thought she caught the faintest hint of a rebuke in them.

But Cora just dimpled adorably and waved.

Isaac shook the reins wordlessly, and the buggy rolled off.

Cora twined one arm around her sister-in-law, and pulled off her bonnet with the other, letting her bright hair spill freely over her shoulders. "Oh, that feels *so* good," she sighed, shaking her head. "I always feel so *smothered* under that awful thing!"

"Joseph and the boys will be in from the fields any minute," Katie told her. "You have time to get settled into your room before we eat. We kept your room the same from your last visit."

"You're an angel, Katie," Cora smiled, and kissed her. "I'll dump my things upstairs and come down to help you set up."

Katie watched her sister-in-law skip up the stairs with an expression of affection, and more than a little trepidation.

***

When Joseph walked through the door thirty minutes later, Cora was seated at the kitchen table, and was just putting the finishing touches on Emma's elegant new French braid. When Cora saw him there, she bounced up and threw herself into his arms.

"Oh, Joes, it's so good to be back again!" she cried.

Joseph laughed and lifted her up in a big bear hug, as if she was still six years old. "Well, she's here at last!" He gave her a sound kiss. "Come and tell me everything that's happened since you left, sprout. We'll have old home week."

"I would have been here earlier, except Daed couldn't spare the buggy and I had to walk. But then Isaac Muller saw me walking and gave me a lift on his way home," Cora told him, sitting back down.

"Oh, he did, did he?" Joseph replied, looking over at Katie.

"Yes, Isaac is always so thoughtful," Katie hastened to add, pouring her husband a glass of coffee. "We should have the Mullers over for dinner sometime."

"That would be lovely," Cora agreed, taking a plate from Katie. "Oh, Joes, you'll never guess. Mamm must have told Fannie Stoltzfus that I was looking for a job. Last Sunday she pulled me to one side and offered me a job as a *teacher's assistant* at the school!"

Conversation at the table died abruptly. All heads turned, and everyone was momentarily speechless.

Katie recovered first. "Well, that's – wonderful, isn't it?" she asked brightly, quelling the children with a look that almost formed the words, *Don't say anything.*

"Yes, I couldn't believe it myself," Cora confessed. "Imagine – me, a teacher!" she laughed.

"I think you'd make a fine teacher," Katie assured her.

"That's what Mrs. Stoltzfus said," Cora replied, munching a biscuit. "But I can't see it."

"I hope you do become a teacher," Caleb piped up. "You're *fun.* Mrs. Stoltzfus is just *old*, and her daughter Mary reminds me of a skinny little chicken."

"*Caleb*!" Katie and Joseph exclaimed, at once.

Cora giggled a little. "Don't scold him," she sputtered. "She *is* kind of a strange bird. Always with her nose in a book!"

"Teachers are *supposed* to read," Joseph reminded her sternly. "And Caleb, if I catch you saying another unkind thing about your teachers, you know what you can expect."

Caleb slumped in his chair. "The corner seat, *all morning*," he replied, with the air of a man resigned to his fate.

"That's right," Joseph reminded him. He turned to Cora. "And you, Cora, you need to remember that not every girl is as... *blessed* as you are. Comparing one person to another is sinful. *Hochmut*."

"Oh, don't be cross with me, Joes, I've only just got here. Don't I get a grace period for at least a few days?"

Joseph looked at her grimly, and cleared his throat.

"Oh, go ahead, Aunt Cora, become our teacher," Jeremy pleaded. "We'll get all A's then, right?" he winked.

"Wrong," Joseph told him, throwing a napkin at his head.

"Well, Cora, at least you'll have one job option this summer," Katie jumped in. "And it might be fun, at least for awhile."

Cora sipped her tea thoughtfully, remembering the

previous Sunday. "It might be. It was very nice of Mrs. Stoltzfus to offer, anyway. She really saved my…"

She broke off, coughed, and fell silent. Katie and Joseph exchanged another wordless look.

***

That evening, when dinner was over and prayers had been said, and all the children were scrubbed and tucked in, Katie sat at her dresser, brushing her hair. Joseph came in and closed the door behind him.

"Everyone socked in?" Katie smiled.

"I was just talking to Cora," Joseph sighed. "I think she really *is* happy to be back."

"Of course she is. She adores you," Katie agreed, and smiled at him.

He sat down on the bed, hands clasped. "Do you really think Cora and Isaac are seeing each other, Kate?"

Katie put down the brush. "Yes. Why?"

He turned his head away. "I don't know. I just don't know what to hope anymore."

Katie put her brush away and sat down on the bed beside him. "Isaac is *good* for her, Joseph," she whispered. "He might even bring her back to God. We're going to have to trust him. I don't think he'll let us down."

"It's not Isaac I'm worried about," Joseph mumbled.

Katie kissed his ear. "You've done enough worrying for one night," she told him. "Come to bed."

"My beautiful bride," he sighed gratefully. "I'm just about ready to fall down tonight."

"Come, then."

They settled into bed, kissed, and turned down the lamps. Five minutes later, Joseph's heavy breathing told Katie that he was fast asleep.

But she lay awake in the darkness for close to an hour, unable to turn off her thoughts. The old house settled in the cool night air, giving off small *pops* and *creaks*. Katie listened with a mother's ear for any sounds from the children's rooms, far down the hall. There were none.

But just when sleep was beginning to feather down over her eyelids, the stealthy sound of a door opening roused her. Soft, light feet went padding down the hall to the back stairway.

Katie bit her lip, then shook Joseph. "Joseph, wake up," she whispered.

He grumbled and rubbed his eyes. "Is there something wrong?"

Katie raised herself up on one elbow and peered out of the window beside their bed. "Look," she whispered.

Joseph looked out of the window. The light over their back porch betrayed Cora as she ran out into the darkness.

Katie could feel Joseph's lips tighten to a straight line. "Well, it looks like you were right. And the *grace period* is officially over."

He threw the covers back and prepared to get dressed. "I have to put a stop to this," he growled. "I can't let my sister slip out after midnight to go and meet a man!"

Katie put her hands up on his chest. "Joseph, don't follow her," she pleaded. "If they're determined, you can't stop them from seeing each other. And better Isaac than anyone else."

This made Joseph pause. He looked out of the window again, glowering. Finally he pulled his hands over his face. "They'd better be getting engaged soon," he said at last. "I'm giving them until the end of the summer."

"Or *what?*" Katie replied in astonishment, stifling a laugh.

"Or – I'll do something. I just don't know what yet," he grumbled.

"Well, the children are asleep and Cora's gone now," his wife replied. "That means *we* finally have some time to *ourselves.*" She tugged on his hand. "*You* may not be sure what *you're* going to do, but I know what *I'm* going to do."

Joseph sighed, and sat glumly on the edge of the bed. Katie's arms twined around him from behind. His frown gradually faded, and was replaced by a rueful, crooked grin.

"Oh, you only think about one thing these days," he complained -- but turned, and went smiling into her arms.

CHAPTER FOUR

The new grass was soft under Cora's bare feet as she ran across the lawn to meet Isaac. It was a beautiful night. A million stars were twinkling in the evening sky, and the air was still warm. The first crickets were beginning to hum softly in the grass.

"*Isaac!*" she called softly.

"I'm here."

Cora followed the sound of his voice over to the old wooden swing in the far corner of Joseph's back yard. Isaac was sitting there quietly, a large, familiar shadow, with his big hands folded on his knees. She snuggled in beside him and lifted her face for a kiss.

But Isaac didn't kiss her. He was quiet.

She looked up at him. "Is something wrong, Isaac?"

He said nothing, and Cora snuggled in deeper. "Tell me,

don't be shy," she prodded. "Did something bad happen at your work?"

"No," he replied. "No, Cora."

"What, then?" she asked innocently.

"Cora, I don't like meeting in secret like this," he said quietly. "I felt bad with Katie today. This isn't right."

She moved again to kiss him, but he refused to turn his face toward her.

She gave an exasperated sigh. "This is the only way we can see each other alone," she objected. "You know that. Oh, Isaac, I'd go crazy if I couldn't talk to you!"

He turned toward her in the darkness. "Is that what I am to you, Cora?" he asked. "A way to stay sane?"

"Of *course* not," Cora replied, stung. "What's come over you tonight, Isaac?"

"I don't know," he shrugged, looking down at his hands. "It's just that... I had hoped you'd know what you wanted to do by now."

Cora pulled back from him. "Oh, that's what everybody says," she replied. "They all want me to be sure, *right now*. Well, I'm *not*, okay? I don't know who I am, Isaac," she pleaded. "I'm reminded every day! I'm not quite Amish, and I'm not quite English. I need time to think."

"And what happens in the meantime?" Isaac asked.

"I don't know," Cora replied. "Does something *have* to happen? Aren't you happy the way things are?"

"No, Cora. I'm not," he answered quietly.

Cora's eyes widened. "You never complained before," she gasped. "You mean that all these times we've been seeing each other, you were *unhappy*?"

"I didn't say that."

"Well, you're saying it now," Cora pointed out.

"Cora, you know what I mean," Isaac told her. "I don't like meeting *this way*."

"Well, you don't have to meet with me at all, if you think it's *wrong*," she replied irritably.

To her surprise, Isaac replied: "I *do* think it's wrong."

"*Oh!*" Cora gasped as if something had knocked the air out of her lungs. It had never occurred to her that Isaac might disapprove of her. She hadn't realized until now how much she depended on him.

Or how much his disapproval *hurt*.

To her horror, she felt her lower lip quivering like a baby's. It was a sure sign that she was about to start crying. She tried to hide it, failed, and jumped up to flee, but Isaac caught her hand, held it.

"Cora," he pleaded, "please don't go."

To Cora's mortification, she burst into tears, and Isaac folded her instantly into his arms. She clung to him, to the protective embrace she had come to associate with all that was safe and good.

Isaac was her surest ally, the one who had always been in her corner. She was able to be strong when she needed to be, mostly because she knew she could always go to Isaac with her hurts.

The thought that he might be angry with her, or even *disappointed*, was so unexpected and crushing that she had no defense against it.

"*Don't*, Cora," he soothed, kissing her hair. "*Don't*. I'm sorry."

"You're *mad* at me!" she cried, in a tone of disbelief.

"I'm not mad."

"You *disapprove* of me!"

"You know that isn't true."

"Do, you, think, I'm, evil, too?" Cora sobbed, her chin bobbing on his chest.

Isaac ran one hand through his shock of hair, distracted. "*Evil?*" he frowned. "Of course not!"

"Everybody else does," Cora cried. "They all think I'm a

floozy, like those women in the old west with the feathers, and they're saying that I'm *corrupting* you with my *brazen lures*!"

Isaac looked up at the sky in disbelief. "Are you *sure?*" he asked.

"Oh, Isaac, you just don't know," she wept.

"I haven't heard *anyone* say those things," he assured her.

"Oh, of *course* they wouldn't say them in front of you!" Cora wailed, and then fell into fresh sobbing.

"Come and sit down," Isaac told her, pulling her back to the swing. He took one shirt cuff and gently dabbed her wet face. "*Don't* cry, Cora. I didn't mean to hurt you. I just meant…well, don't worry about what I meant."

"Why do you think it's *wrong* to see me, Isaac?" Cora whispered. "We haven't done anything we shouldn't."

"I don't like coming here in the dark, Cora," Isaac replied evenly. "I don't like courting you in secret. No, I don't like *courting* any more at all. *I want us to be…*"

Cora felt her mouth dropping open in amazement. She put her hand quickly to his lips, and his words trailed off into silence. His lips were hot under her fingertips, as if they were burning with those unspoken words.

Cora's pulse jumped up into her throat and did an odd, excited dance. Isaac was asking to *marry her*.

She sat there, hardly daring to breathe, questioning her heart. She should be *delirious* with joy.

But for some reason, the thought filled her not with joy, but with terror. She couldn't go there, not yet. She wasn't *ready* for that, even if Isaac was.

So she looked off into the distance, to the steady, yellow light from the Muller's farm, far away. The deep silence of night stretched out between her and Isaac. After a while, she piped up, a little too brightly:

"You'd never guess, Isaac, Fannie Stoltzfus offered me a job as an assistant teacher the other day. At the school," she sniffed, wiping her eyes with one hand.

Isaac was quiet for a long while, and finally replied, brokenly: "That... that sounds good. Are you going to accept the job?"

"Do you *want* me to accept it, Isaac?" she asked softly. For now at least, it was the best she could offer him.

But, being Isaac, he took the offering. He raised his head, looked at her intently.

"Yes, Cora. I think I would."

Her voice quavered. "All right, Isaac. If *you* want me to take the job, I will." She smiled at him crookedly.

Isaac put out his hand and caressed her cheek. Then he pulled her into his arms and gave her a long, tender kiss that told her that he had no anger in him.

And his second kiss added all the other things that she had not allowed him to say.

***

When Cora finally returned to her bedroom, an hour later, she walked to the window and gazed out across the moonlit fields. She imagined Isaac making the dark, chilly trek back home and thought how discouraged and rejected he must feel. He had tried to ask her to *marry* him tonight, and she had stopped him.

She suddenly felt ashamed. This *wasn't* fair to him. And even though it hurt her that Isaac had objected to their meetings, he was right. They *were* taking a terrible risk. It was getting harder and harder to send him away. It was getting easier and easier to go a little farther every time they kissed.

If they kept meeting this way, sooner or later they were going to go too far. If tonight was any guide, *very* soon.

Cora sighed. It was no longer a question of whether she wanted Isaac – she *wanted* him. She was more than half convinced that she loved him enough to marry him.

But if she married him, she'd be looking across these same fields most every day for the rest of her life. And once she joined the church – *if* she joined – there would be no going back, no second chances.

If she messed up *then*, she could lose everything – her parents, Joes and Katie, all her family.

And the awful possibility she could barely make herself admit: *she might lose Isaac.* Or worse, he'd come with her to the English, and be miserable for the rest of his life.

She kicked off her shoes, suddenly angry. Why did life have to be so hard, so black and white? Why did God demand so much?

She looked up at the serene night sky. *Aren't You supposed to love him, too?* she asked impatiently, and threw herself onto the bed.

There was no answer from the sky, no sudden inspiration to tell her what to do. Just the growing conviction that maybe, it would be best for Isaac if she stopped sending him secret invitations to meet with her. Maybe they should stop seeing each other altogether, at least until she was sure of what she wanted.

Which, Cora thought unhappily, was probably the right thing, the *Amish* thing to do. If she'd been a good Amish person, she supposed that doing the right thing should give her at least *some* satisfaction.

But she must be *very* selfish and evil, because the idea only resulted in more tears.

CHAPTER FIVE

At five o'clock the next morning, Caleb Lapp scanned the bleary faces around the breakfast table, and blurted: "Everybody looks so *tired* this morning!" His bright eyes rested on his father. "Are you *sick*, daed? You look the worst of all!"

Joseph Lapp glared at his hapless son. Then his eyes moved to his wife, who was wearing an innocent look; then they moved to Cora, and rested grimly on her face for a few moments. He said nothing.

"Everyone bow their heads for prayer," Katie interjected quickly. "Joseph?"

Joseph bowed his head. "Oh Lord, thank you for this new day and – " he looked sidelong at Cora – "getting us all *safely through the night.*"

Cora frowned slightly, but didn't open her eyes.

"We thank you for Your many blessings: our loved ones, work for our hands to do, a roof over our heads. Thank you for helping us keep our hearts open, and our *consciences clear.*"

Cora opened her eyes, glanced sidelong at him, and closed them again.

"Thank you for the refreshment of *sleep,* and *adequate rest,* so that we have enough strength to face the new day, and all of its... *challenges.*"

Katie frowned slightly, but didn't open her eyes.

"We may feel, sometimes, as though we're about to fall *face down into the dirt,* but give us the grace to use our *last ounce of strength* to keep going, even though we may feel *tested* to the point of *death.*

"Amen."

But there was no answering *amen.* The children were staring at their father, jaws agape.

"Eat your eggs, Caleb," Katie told him, patting his hand.

As soon as the meal was over, Joseph and the older boys left for the fields. Joseph paused on the threshold, gave his wife a significant look, and stalked out with the wounded air of the unjustly persecuted.

Both Katie and Cora received this unspoken comment with apparent serenity.

"Caleb, help Emma clean up the dishes," Katie instructed the children. "I'm going to town, and I'm taking Cora with me."

She took Cora's hand and led her outside to the porch. The sun had just crowned the low hills beyond their fields, and the air smelled fresh and clean.

"Walk with me," Katie told her.

They started off down the road, walking down the long dirt track into town at a leisurely pace. It was a three-mile stroll, not too far, and a pleasant excursion on such a morning. The countryside was still covered in dew and silence. The new sun broke through the low mists in the hollows, turning the fields green and gold.

"Joes seemed a little tense this morning," Cora said at last.

"Don't mind him. He's cranky because..." Katie looked down, smiled, and bit her lip. "He's working a lot of jobs these days."

They walked in silence for awhile. The road to town took them past the Muller farm, and they were now on the outskirts of the Muller's pastures. There was no one out working them yet. Cora pulled her shawl around her shoulders, grateful that Isaac had a job in town, and that she was spared the sight of him working in the fields. It was a sight that she always found oddly sensual, and after last night, she wasn't equal to *more* temptation.

She looked up to see Katie's eyes on her. "I can always tell when you're thinking about Isaac Muller," Katie said unexpectedly. "Your eyes just come alive. They practically change color."

Cora gaped at her sister-in-law in dismay, wondering if her thoughts were that obvious to *everyone*. She felt herself going red. "Isaac is a good friend," she stammered. "I was… just thinking about how nice he was, to offer me a lift the other day."

Katie looked down. "Yes, Isaac is one in a million," she agreed. "Men with his kind of integrity are rare."

Cora looked at her sharply, prepared to be defensive; but Katie's eyes were soft, and her expression mild. Cora slowly let her defenses drop.

"Yes. That's true," she admitted.

"I think I'm going to invite the Mullers over for dinner soon," Katie replied. "Do you think Isaac would come, too?"

"He might," Cora replied noncommittally.

"If you see him again, would you ask him, for me?" Katie asked blandly.

"All right," Cora sighed, and glanced off across the fields again. She said nothing, but she was thinking, bitterly, that if seeing *less* of Isaac was the right thing to do, then the universe was making that very hard for her.

***

To Cora's chagrin, when they reached town, Katie took her straight to Elie Meissen's store. Elie was famous -- or infamous -- for her love of gossip.

"You go ahead," Cora told her sister-in-law. "I'll stay out here and wait for you."

Cora figured that if *Katie* could read her face like a signpost, there was no telling what the sharp-eyed store manager, Elie, would see there.

"All right," Katie smiled, and disappeared into the small clapboard building.

The Meissens had added a small dry goods section to their store, and on that morning, it was busy. There was already a line for the community phone, and the small building was filled with customers.

The town was fairly busy, too. Cora's eyes were drawn across the street and down a few doors, to the cabinet-making shop where she knew Isaac was working. He was an apprentice now, but would soon be a full-fledged cabinet maker. He had always been wonderful with wood. Cora smiled, remembering how as a child, Isaac had once made her a little heart with her name carved into it.

She looked up at the shop again, and now her heart jumped up into her throat. Isaac had appeared in the doorway, as if he had been conjured up by her thoughts, and the sight of him sent her pulse racing. He looked around, and over, and then up – to where she was standing.

He froze. They stared at one another for a long moment. Then his lips pursed together. Cora had seen that expression before; it was what happened when Isaac clenched his jaw.

He stepped out into the street, eyes on her, and took three big strides in the direction of the store. Cora held her breath.

Then the store door swung open, and something dark and fast-moving brushed past Cora's shoulder from behind.

"Well, hello Isaac!"

To Cora's amazement, Leah Hauser flounced *right in front of her* and intercepted Isaac as he crossed the street. Cora's brows rushed together.

What the devil, she thought in irritation. Leah was smiling, her face half-turned. Cora thought bitterly that Leah had done it so she could enjoy *her* confusion, as well as Isaac's. Leah was holding – what was it? – some kind of basket. The brazen cow – now she actually had her *hand on Isaac's arm!*

Isaac stopped mid-stride, looked down at Leah, mumbled a few words, shot a look over at Cora.

Cora became aware that she was gripping the porch rail,

and she let it go. She put one hand up to her hair, yanking off her bonnet. If Leah Hauser wanted to pick a fight with her, she was about to succeed beyond her wildest dreams.

Cora stepped out into the street and was rolling up her sleeves when something bumped into her, *hard*.

She rounded on the offender with fire in her eyes. But to her confusion, it was nobody but scrawny little Mary Stoltzfus, come to shop at the store.

Mary looked up at her with her ridiculously serious green eyes. "Oh… excuse me," she said, in a dead-level voice, and without even the ghost of a smile.

Cora backpedaled, overbalanced. In her confusion, she and almost fell down.

"Watch out for the steps," Mary warned her.

Cora's grabbed for the porch rail and righted herself. Then her eyes rolled to the spot where Isaac had been, but in just those few seconds, he had disappeared. Now there was no sign of either Isaac *or* Leah. Cora almost ground her teeth in frustration.

Cora became aware that Mary Stoltzfus was still staring at her, but she made no attempt to recover her temper. "Why don't you watch where you're going!" she snapped.

Mary looked at her again, then entered the store without another word.

Cora trained a green glance on the cabinet shop. What was Leah Hauser doing inside? The witch had no relatives there, no plausible errand, no believable excuse.

She was *hunting* Isaac, pure and simple.

Cora bit her lip. Should she march across the street, burst into the shop and drag Leah Hauser out by the hair? It was what she *wanted* to do.

And then, for an encore, she'd go back into the store and dump a pail of water of Mary Stoltzfus' clumsy little head.

The store door opened behind her, and Katie appeared at her elbow. "I'm done here," Katie told her cheerfully. "Do you have any business in town, Cora?"

Then she took a look at Cora's face, and her voice trailed off.

Cora took a deep breath. Katie's calm, rational voice reminded her of Joes. She had already caused poor Joes a world of trouble. She imagined herself trying to explain why she had started a brawl in the middle of town, and closed her eyes.

"No... no, I don't have any business here," she said at last.

But as they walked away, she kept her eyes on the cabinet shop until the bend of the road completely obscured it from sight.

They walked back home in silence. Cora's eyes wandered

over the Muller's fields as they passed. It was no doubt *wrong, selfish*, and utterly *un-Amish*, but her noble resolve to stay away from Isaac had gone up in a puff of infernal fire.

Suddenly she piped up: "You know, I'm sure that the Mullers would *love* to have dinner with us. Maybe I'll walk over and invite them."

Katie looked down at her feet and pinched in a smile. She walked for awhile in silence, and then replied: "Why don't you? I won't tell Joseph."

Cora looked over at Katie, searched her face.

"Thank you, Katie," she said softly.

Her eyes lingered on Katie's face, and her expression lightened. "You know, you're looking very happy this morning," she added, impulsively grabbing her sister-in-law's hand. "Did you buy something *extravagant* at the store?"

Katie smiled more deeply, shook her head. "No -- just what we needed."

"What *did* you buy?" Cora peeked into the brown paper bag. There was thread, buttons, a packet of hooks and eyes, and a big, fluffy ball of soft white yarn.

Cora looked down at the ball of yarn, and looked up at Katie again. Her sister-in-law suddenly went bright red, and couldn't meet her eyes.

Cora blinked at her. Then light dawned visibly across her

face.

"Oh, *Katie*," she whispered, and then burst out laughing. "Does Joes know yet?"

Katie shook her head, smiling.

"No wonder Joes has been looking tired," Cora giggled. "Wait until he hears!

"Congratulations!"

Cora threw her arms around her blushing sister-in-law, and laughed again.

CHAPTER SIX

Katie Lapp sat in front of her dresser, calmly brushing her long brown hair. Her husband was splayed out over their bed with his hands over his eyes.

After a long while he pulled his hands down over his face and rolled his eyes over at his wife.

"You haven't said anything for a long time," he commented.

Katie smiled and shook her head slightly. "I didn't want to bother you," she said softly. "I know you're tired."

"Thank you."

He put his arms behind his head and closed his eyes, but soon opened them again.

"Anything *new* in town today?"

She shook her head. "No."

"No news with the children?"

She smiled again. "They're all fine."

He fell silent again. He strummed his brown finger on the quilt, looked over at her.

"You're not coming to bed?"

"Not yet."

He digested this. "There's nothing *wrong*, is there?"

"Why, of course not. Why do you ask?"

"Well, usually you're all over me by now," he replied frankly, looking at her with trepidation. "Are you tired tonight?"

"Not especially."

"What then?"

She put the brush down and turned to look at him. "I'm trying to be generous," she smiled. "Go to sleep, Joseph. I can see that you're tired."

He reclined on the bed and closed his eyes, but frowned and opened them again and looked over at her. His blue eyes were soft and contrite.

"I'm sorry, Kate," he told her softly. "I've been meaning to tell you all day. I was harsh with you and Cora this morning."

"I wasn't angry."

"They were wrong, those things I said."

Katie stopped brushing her hair, rose and went to her husband. His arms reached for her, and she sat on the bed beside him.

"You have the patience of an angel, and I love you," she told him. She leaned down and kissed him.

"Come to bed, then."

Katie climbed in beside Joseph and pillowed on his chest. They stayed there in silence for a long while.

Joseph finally sighed in exasperation. "Kate, there's *something*. Last night, every night for a month, you are a menace. *Tonight*, no kisses, no giggling, no fingers doing the walking. What?"

Katie snuggled deeper into his chest and smiled. "I thought you were the little deer that only wants to escape the *hunter*," she teased.

He looked down at her, and finally admitted: "Well… for someone who wants to escape, the little deer gets caught a lot."

"It's true," she agreed, smiling. "And it looks like the little deer got caught once too often."

She looked up at him.

Joseph's blue eyes widened. He sat up straight, ran one

hand through his hair. Then he caught Katie up in his arms, and laughed so loudly that the whole house was wakened.

***

The next morning the Lapp children ate their breakfast in ominous silence. Joseph and Katie were more than usually strange. They had come down to breakfast so late that everyone else had already finished eating. They smiled and laughed and made calf's eyes at one another until the boys began to make furtive gagging gestures.

Even Caleb watched his parents with irritated bemusement. Finally, the six-year-old thumped the table with his fists and demanded: "Okay, what's *wrong* with you people?"

Katie and Joseph froze mid-kiss, stared at him, and then burst out laughing.

Joseph drew himself up for an announcement. "Children, Katie and I have something to tell you." He reached for Katie's hand.

"Katie and I are expecting a baby. You're going to have a little brother or sister!"

There was stunned silence for a split-second, shattered when Emma shrieked "Oh, Katie!" and threw herself into Katie's arms.

The boys digested the news in stolid silence. Their expressions said: *Well, that explains it.*

But Caleb's big round eyes were like blue marbles.

"You mean *instead of me?*" he wailed.

Katie's expression was instantly stricken. Her arms reached for him. "No, no, Caleb," she soothed him, as he climbed into her lap for comfort. She kissed his hair. "No new baby could ever take the place of our Caleb."

"You'll have a new brother or sister to play with," Joseph told him reassuringly.

Caleb looked over at Jeremy and Hezekiah, and seemed unconvinced.

"You can be the *big* brother now," Katie whispered in his ear. "Not the *baby*."

Caleb seemed struck by this. He sat up in her arms. "Hey – that's right!" He looked over at his father, who nodded confirmation.

"You're getting to be a *man* now," he told Caleb gravely. "You're too *big* to be the *youngest* anymore."

Caleb considered this, and then pushed out of Katie's lap and climbed back into his chair. Katie turned swimming eyes to Joseph, who squeezed her hand.

Cora slipped up quietly behind Joseph, put her arms around her brother, and kissed his ear. "I'm so happy for you and Katie, Joes," she told him.

He half-turned. "You didn't seem very surprised," he smiled.

"We all have our little secrets," she teased, and then wished she'd chosen her words more carefully. But to her relief, for *that* morning at least, Joseph had no room in his mind for anything but joy. He laughed, and patted her cheek with one hand, and then turned back to Katie.

***

Since it seemed that the work day had officially derailed, and probably indefinitely, Cora slipped out onto the front porch. It was another beautiful day dawning, a weekend morning.

Isaac would be at home.

Cora glanced back over her shoulder, listening to the happy chatter and laughter inside. No one would miss her for awhile yet. She smiled, slipped off her shoes, and padded soundlessly across the lawn, around the side of the house, and out across the fields to the fence between the two farms.

Her feet were wet with dew when she reached the little brook. Golden morning beams slanted through the trees, painted the air with blocks of gold. Far across the green meadows, she could hear the small sounds of life stirring, the start of the work day: a door slamming, horse hooves, the clink of tackle.

This spot, where the brook whispered and the leaves were cool, was where Matt had almost killed her. But on this beautiful morning, the place held no evil memories for Cora. It was once again the place where she and Isaac had played as children, and where they had kissed many times since.

She looked up. Even from this distance, she recognized him. Isaac, in his plain straw hat and his white shirt and black slacks. He was doing some chore out in the fields, unaware of her gaze.

Cora's expression softened. Yes, she loved him -- how could she not? He was sweet and faithful and handsome and strong, and in that instant, Cora felt ready to run across the field like a mad thing and tell him that she would marry him right away.

But she hesitated, and the impulse passed. She sighed, smiled, shook her head, and merely climbed over the fence.

It took him awhile to notice her as she walked across the fields. He was intent on his work, looking down. She watched him as she walked, how broad his shoulders looked, the strength of his arms, the way he worked.

There was something about the sight that always made Cora's mind wander inappropriately. It never failed to make her mouth go dry. How young and strong Isaac was -- and how sweetly unconscious of his looks.

Cora raised her hand. "Isaac!"

He took off his hat, looked around.

"Isaac!"

Then he saw her, and his whole aspect changed. He straightened suddenly, met her eyes, squared his shoulders.

Cora smiled. That was as close to preening as Isaac would ever get, but she knew his body language.

"Isaac."

She held out her hand, still clutching a daisy that she had pulled up from the meadow. "Can you talk with me?"

Isaac dropped his tools. "Sure."

"Come down to the creek," Cora urged. "I have news."

She reached down and took his hand, and he followed her without a backward glance. She swung the daisy back and forth as they walked.

"What did Leah Hauser want yesterday?" she asked, trying to make her voice sound casual.

He shot her a quick look from under his hat. "Nothing. She wanted my opinion about a pie, or something."

"*Hmm*," Cora nodded, careful to keep her eyes on the far horizon. "I just wondered. You looked like you wanted to say something to *me* beforehand," she added.

He was silent, and she looked over at him.

"You don't have to tell me if you don't want," she added softly. Then she brightened.

"But I have news for you. Katie wants you and your parents to come over for dinner."

This time Isaac looked up. His expression was one of relief.

"I'm sure they'll be glad to, and you know I will," he assured her.

They had reached the fence that divided the farms, and Isaac lifted her up and over as if she weighed nothing at all. Then he clambered over, and they sat together on the low branch of a massive oak overshadowing the water.

"The plan was for next week, but I don't know if it still is. Katie and Joes are distracted this morning." Cora dimpled in delight.

Isaac squeezed her hand. "It must be something good," he told her. "You look happy."

"We're all happy," she smiled. "Don't tell anybody yet, but *Katie's pregnant.*"

Isaac's face registered astonishment, followed by genuine pleasure. "That's *great*, Cora. I'm happy for them."

His smile faded. His gaze lingered, softened. Cora felt her cheeks going red, because she could see that Isaac was imagining *her* as a mother – the mother of their own children.

She looked down quickly.

He put his hand under her chin and lifted it until she looked up. He smiled again, wistfully. "Tell Katie and Joes that we'll be come over for dinner. *And that I'm happy for them.*"

Cora smiled, and promised, and couldn't help kissing him. And just for an instant, she allowed herself to share the pretty fantasy that she'd surprised in his eyes.

She saw herself holding a baby, Isaac's baby – a beautiful blue-eyed baby, with white-blonde hair.

CHAPTER SEVEN

"No one is questioning your good intentions," Berta Eckhard was saying. "Everyone in the community knows your compassion, Fannie."

"It's just that – well, you know the rumors that are flying around about Cora Lapp," Elizabeth Hauser added. "She was mixed up in a *murder*, if the news reports are to be believed. She was living with a thief, a *criminal*. She helped him to commit a crime and almost paid with her own life." Mrs. Hauser sniffed and put her teacup to her lips.

Fannie Stoltzfus sat stiffly in her living room, balancing a plate on her lap and holding a teacup in her hand as her neighbors bombarded her with questions.

The room was electric with tension.

"Should someone like *that* be teaching our children?" Mrs. Eckhard pressed. "A teacher must be an *example* to our youth. The only example Cora Lapp has given is of…"

Mrs. Stoltzfus interrupted her. "I know the stories about Cora's rumspringa," she countered. "But I've been watching her since she was a little girl in my schoolroom. I think she would be a better teacher than anyone guesses."

"But she'll have no credibility with the children," Mrs. Hauser objected. "What can she teach them about *obedience* and *modesty*? You can't teach what you don't know! Cora Lapp hasn't even joined the *church* yet!

"Then, too, the older children know her story, and the girls – well, they won't have anything to do with her, and I'm sure I don't wonder."

"And what about your *own* daughter?" Mrs. Eckhard asked, in a lower voice. "It isn't fair to her. *Mary* is the natural choice to replace you. She's been helping you for years!"

"Mary is a wonderful assistant," Mrs. Stoltzfus replied softly, "and she's like my right hand. But there's no harm in having two assistants. They might complement each other. Mary is reliable and knowledgeable. Cora is spontaneous and might help the children see that learning can be fun."

Mrs. Hauser snorted. "The kind of *fun* Cora Lapp can teach about isn't the kind that I want *my* children to learn!"

Fannie Stoltzfus' voice became cold. "I've already made her the offer," she replied, in a tone of finality. "I can't take it back now without breaking my word, and I don't see the necessity in any case. It's a trial offer, after all. Cora may decide that *she* doesn't want it."

"There are a lot of people in this community who wouldn't be unhappy, if things turned out that way," Mrs. Hauser answered crisply. "Well, Fannie, all I can say is that you have a great deal of faith in her. We'll see!"

"Yes, that young hellion is certainly fortunate to have someone with *your* standing to stick up for her," Mrs. Eckhard agreed. "She's put her own family through the wringer – her poor parents, and her brother Joseph – everyone feels so sorry for *him*. There was almost a murder at his house! Of course he can't *help* being related to her, but I hope *you* don't live to regret your decision."

There was a rustling sound, and Mrs. Stoltzfus' visitors rose.

"You know we're just thinking of you, Fannie," Mrs. Hauser said, in a solicitous voice. "We hate to see you get mixed up in a scandal. But you've always had such a soft heart."

"I hope we haven't offended you by speaking plainly," Mrs. Eckhard added. "But we might as well say it, as think it! Give our love to your husband, and to Mary. We'll see you next Sunday."

Then the sound of receding footsteps, and the creak of a screen door, announced that the visitors had gone.

***

Mary Stoltzfus leaned back into the shadows at the top of the stairs. She could hear her mother muttering softly in German downstairs, and the sharp sound of rattling teacups.

She sat on the floor, chewing one stubby fingernail thoughtfully. She didn't especially *like* either one of her mother's visitors, but she wasn't sure they were *wrong*, either.

Mary frowned. Her mother's decision to invite Cora to become her assistant had come as a painful and *total* surprise. Berta Eckhart was right – *she* was the natural choice to become the community's next teacher. *She* had been her mother's helper for years, *she* knew exactly what needed to be done, and *she* loved teaching – and learning.

But so far, Cora Lapp hadn't shown the slightest aptitude for either one. The only thing she seemed to be good at was looking pretty, and upsetting the whole town.

She even seemed to have a *temper*. Mary rubbed her shoulder, remembering how Cora's eyes had blazed when they'd bumped each other at the store.

But that was the way with pretty girls, she'd learned: they seemed to think they were better than everybody else.

***

"Mary?" Her mother's voice came calling from

downstairs. "Are you going to the youth sing on Sunday night?"

Mary bit her lip, wondering if it would be a sin to pretend not to have heard.

"Mary?"

"No, Mamm. I'm going to stay at home and work on my quilt."

"But there will be boys there, and you're on your rumspringa," her mother reminded her.

Mary rolled her eyes. "I know. I'll think about it," she called, and then retreated to her bedroom before her mother could start thinking of *specific* boys.

She flopped down on her bed and pulled a scrapbook out from underneath the mattress. It was covered in pictures that she'd cut out of magazines, places that she dreamed about visiting someday: New York, London, Shanghai, Paris.

Especially Paris.

She ran her fingertips over the photo of the Louvre. It was a magical place, filled with the wealth of kings, with golden treasures and masterpieces.

A place filled with mankind's brightest and best accomplishments. A place where excellence was celebrated and on display for the world to see.

Not labeled as *hochmut* and pushed away as evil.

Mary sighed and ran her fingertips over the magazine photos. She dreamed of going to see it all herself one day, if only she could muster up the nerve to leave home.

She tossed the scrapbook aside and pulled another book from underneath the mattress, a slender workbook entitled, "Learning French in Easy Steps."

"Je suis une juene fille," she mouthed silently, "Je m'appelle Marie."

"Mary?" her mother's voice called again. "You really should get out of the house more, dear. I hope you at least consider going to the sing."

Mary sighed and didn't answer. If only her mother would stop trying to push her!

She *hated* the sings. Other girls might have fun there because they were pretty and there were always plenty of boys to show them attention.

But when *she* went, she always ended up sitting by herself, watching everybody else have fun until some kind soul – usually the chaperone – noticed her there and came over to make conversation.

Her mother had been the chaperone last Sunday and had dragged her to the sing, but it had been an *especially* tiresome ordeal. As usual, she had been pushed to the periphery of conversation, as the other girls huddled together, gossiping about Cora Lapp and her sordid adventure out among the English.

Mary shuddered. Cora's near-fatal disaster only reinforced her own worst fears about the dangers of venturing outside her small community.

She wanted to go, to travel to wonderful places, but all travel involved risk – and danger. The outside world was magical and beautiful, but it could also be dark, frightening, and filled with evil people, as Cora Lapp's near-murder had proven.

Mary's eyes returned longingly to the workbook. If by some miracle she was able to travel to New York or Paris, would she enjoy the magic that the magazines promised?

Or would her inexperience of the world draw predators – as it had with Cora Lapp?

"Mary?" Her mother's voice called again.

Not that it was *ever* going to be more than an academic question.

"I'll be down in a few minutes, Mamm," she called.

Mary sighed. Who was she kidding? She was *never* going to get out of Pennsylvania. She was going to live in this *same* place, her *entire life*. She frowned and stuffed the workbook back under the mattress.

Plus, *now* she was going to have to work with the *golden child*, that *spoiled princess* Cora Lapp, and it was going to be a pain.

Mary wondered briefly if her mother was angry with her. Why else would she bring in a stranger to do *her* job? Why would she saddle her with a vain, empty-headed trainee – who was also, coincidentally, the most unpopular girl in the county?

It was almost like a *punishment*.

And I'm unpopular enough all by myself, Mary thought, with a grimace. I don't need extra help!

"Mary?"

Another French word came to Mary's mind, but she didn't allow herself to speak it.

"Coming, Mamm." She rolled off of her narrow bed and trudged reluctantly down the stairs.

CHAPTER EIGHT

"Scholars, we're going to have a new assistant in the schoolroom," Fannie Stoltzfus smiled. "You all know Cora Lapp, and her family. Cora will be helping us out for a while. Cora, Mary, why don't you come up to the front of the room?"

Mary cringed inside, but slowly walked to the front of the one-room schoolhouse and stood shoulder to shoulder with Cora Lapp. Cora smiled, and Mary stood there and wished she could disappear.

There was stolid silence, punctuated with a few sniffs from the younger children, and some faint whispering from the back of the room, where the oldest ones were sitting.

Mary kept her expression neutral. She was miffed by what felt like a snub from her mother, and didn't like having to stand side by side with the prettiest girl in the county, and having their looks compared, but didn't intend to broadcast her embarrassment to the room.

She tried to avoid making eye contact with Cora. It might be a little mean, but if she didn't make Cora feel too comfortable, maybe she'd quit all on her own and just *go away*.

That was what *other* people were hoping for – why shouldn't *she*?

"Mary, why don't you let Cora follow along as you work. That way she can get a feel for what we're doing," her mother suggested.

Mary stifled a sigh. She addressed Cora over her shoulder: "If you have questions, save them up, and you can ask me after class." She didn't turn to watch Cora's reaction.

Then she went about her daily routine, circulating among the children, explaining this thing, answering that question – and behaving as if Cora didn't exist. It wasn't always easy – the younger children seemed to like Cora right away, and Cora's little nephew Caleb started talking to her and kept nattering on for a long time.

Mary was also aware of her mother's eye on her. She was no doubt going to get a lecture at home over her cool reception of the new assistant -- but what did her mother *expect*?

Her new shadow was silent all through the morning, but at the lunch recess, Mary felt a soft tap on her shoulder. Cora was standing there. She was smiling, but she looked determined.

"I have some questions," she began. "Do you talk to your mother about the lessons before you start? You seem to know just what to say."

Mary shrugged. "That's because I've been helping her for years," she replied flatly. "I know the material."

I practically have it memorized, she added to herself, wondering for the thousandth time what her mother had seen in this silly blonde girl. She knew nothing, she was going to have to be trained from scratch. It made no sense *whatsoever*.

"Will your mother give me something to look at, so I can start learning it, too?" Cora persisted.

Mary stared at her. "You... *could* read the textbooks," she drawled. She was gratified to see that she'd hit a nerve: Cora's cheeks went red, and her jaw clenched slightly.

"I'll just talk to your mother about it," she said, and turned on her heel.

Mary shrugged and went back to straightening up in the classroom. She watched as Cora walked outside to the recess area. She sat down on the edge of the grass and watched as the kids played. None of them came up to talk to her.

Mary felt a twinge of something like guilt, but squashed it. It felt mean, but Cora was never going to make a teacher, and in the end it would be kinder to push her out quickly and have done with it, than to drag things out.

And there was no denying that it would also make her *own* life a lot easier.

***

But as the weeks passed, it became clear -- to Mary's irritation – that Cora wasn't going to *be pushed*.

The first month of Life with Cora felt like one long endurance test to Mary. As she had expected, her mother noticed her coldness toward Cora that first day and, when they got home, had given her a stern lecture that left her feeling hurt and resentful. Her mother had used words like *jealous* and *disappointed*, but Mary couldn't help thinking that her mother might have seen those things coming.

To add to her annoyance, Cora also proved to be somewhat less dense than she had thought: that first day, she'd gone home with an armload of textbooks and had studied them so thoroughly that she had actually started to be of some use.

The knowledge that her *own* snarkiness had probably been the motivation for that, didn't help her mood.

But worst of all, to Mary's mind, was that day by day, the children were starting to open up to Cora – especially the younger ones. She could hardly admit it to herself, but after all her years teaching there, that part *hurt*. She had hoped that at least in *this* arena, the area where she knew the most, where she was *most* useful – that she wouldn't lose out to a pretty face.

Like in all the *other* areas of her life.

Sometimes she got angry. It wasn't *fair*. It wasn't fair that she should lose both her job, *and* the children's affection, to this girl. It wasn't fair that some people were born lucky and got all the breaks in life just because of how they looked, when everybody else had to *perform* to make it.

It felt selfish. Cora didn't *need* a job. Cora could have any boy in the county. The gossip around town was that Isaac Muller was already dying of love for her, and that he wasn't the only one. All Cora had to do to be comfortable in life was to get married, and let her husband take care of her.

But, Mary told herself glumly, there were no boys fighting over *her*. She was going to have to work a job, probably for the rest of her life. She had carved out this one little niche for herself. This was the one thing she could *do*, that she was good at.

And now, it looked like it was going to be taken away. She had no idea what she would do, if she didn't become the next teacher.

***

Of course, there was that *one* thing -- that fantasy of hers, the thing she took solace in when she began to feel down --

the writing.

She had been scribbling secretly for years, unbeknownst to her parents, hiding dog-eared notebooks under the floorboards of her bedroom. There were dozens of them now, all filled with her ridiculous dreams – her dreams of travel, of education, of discovering new things, of becoming a *real* writer.

Even, God help her, of being *pretty*, for once in her life.

She had made one feeble attempt to make them come true: she had seen an essay contest advertised in a magazine, with a first prize of an all-expense paid trip to Paris. It had been so tempting, so glamorous, that she had gone so far as to scribble out an entry and stick it into an envelope.

But her chances of winning were ridiculously small, and so her entry was still lying in an envelope under her bed. The trip to Paris still haunted her dreams, but a *dream* was all it was, in the end.

And so the envelope stayed under her bed, gathering dust. Mary told herself that her pessimism was grounded solidly in experience.

In the real world, plain-Jane Amish girls just didn't have *that* kind of luck.

CHAPTER NINE

"Come in everyone, make yourselves comfortable!"

Joseph opened the front door and for an instant, the light from outside was blocked, because Theodor, Adie, and Isaac Muller walked in. Theodor Muller was so tall that he barely cleared the doorway, and his wife Adie was only slightly less so. Isaac, at his towering six feet plus, was actually the shortest person in his family.

All three of the Mullers had thick white hair: Theodor because he was on the high side of fifty, and Adie and Isaac because near-white blonde was their natural hair color. Even in middle age, Adie was a tall, dignified woman with beautiful features and a flawless porcelain complexion. She wore a crown of braids atop her head, and even without a speck of makeup, was still a striking woman.

Katie accepted the gift of homemade muscadine wine that Adie offered her, then wiped her hands on a dish towel and welcomed her guests to the big living room. Theodor and

Adie settled on the couch, and Isaac sat down in a big stuffed chair by the fireplace. Cora stepped up, offering the Mullers tea and coffee and a round of cookies.

The girls shuttled back and forth from the kitchen, putting the finishing touches on the epic feast that Katie had spent all day preparing. The entire house was suffused with the heavenly aroma of baked bread, cake, coconut pie, biscuits, sugar-glazed ham, fried chicken, cheesy potato casseroles and all kinds of vegetables swimming in butter. The big kitchen table was so full of platters and plates and cups that there was literally no room left for even one more dish.

As she worked, Cora stole little glances at Isaac. He filled Joseph's big stuffed chair, and suddenly looked so grown up and adult that she wondered why she hadn't noticed the change before. He was almost as tall as Joseph now, and would soon be making his own way in the world. She felt a little glow of pride in him. Isaac would soon be his own man in the community, and would be a *fine* addition to it.

She also began to understand why Isaac had wanted this, and why Katie had volunteered to do it. It *was* nice to be able to see Isaac's parents up close, and to let them see her. She hoped they'd look at her in a positive light, as a person who was at least *trying* to fit in and make Isaac happy.

So she stayed quiet as her elders talked. Joes and Mr. Muller discussed the farming prospects, and Katie and Mrs. Muller talked about the news in town, and recent family doings.

Theodor motioned toward his son. "Isaac is the one making news nowadays," he told Joseph. "He's almost finished with his apprenticeship. He'll be starting with Hans Miller at the cabinet shop next month."

Katie turned to Isaac. "Isaac has always turned out such beautiful work," she smiled. "I've seen some of the things he's done – he has a real gift."

Isaac looked down at his feet, but Cora could see that he was pleased by the compliment. "I'll be at home for awhile at first, of course, but I mean to build my *own* house as soon as I can," he replied, looking at Joseph.

Joseph nodded. "Hans is lucky to have you, Isaac. I know you'll do well."

Cora smiled, blessing Joes silently for that affirmation, and then grabbed the coffee jug and went to refill Isaac's empty cup. She caught his eye as she bent over him, smiled, and was gratified to see by his expression that he got the message as surely as if she'd said it aloud: *I'm proud of you.*

"Is everyone ready for dinner?" Katie asked.

Emma called the children in, and soon everyone was at the kitchen table. Cora hung back, because she didn't want Isaac's parents to think ill of her for grabbing the spot next to Isaac, but Isaac held out his hand for her in front of everyone. She felt herself going red, and shot a glance at Isaac's mother before sitting down beside him.

Cora furtively scanned the faces at the table, but no one seemed to take any undue notice of Isaac's gesture, so she allowed herself to relax. She looked up at Isaac, but he only smiled and squeezed her hand under the table.

Katie's cooking was always delicious, and Cora noticed with amusement that Isaac's hearty appetite was the same as ever. For some reason, it gave her real pleasure to see him enjoy his meal, and she couldn't help imagining what it would be to cook for him every day. She hadn't been able to resist baking his favorite – sawdust pie – herself.

To her relief, Katie pointed this out *for* her.

"Does anyone have room for pie?" she asked, her eyes on Isaac. "Cora made the pecan pie herself, and I think it turned out really well."

Isaac's face brightened. "I love sawdust pie!" he laughed, and held out his plate. Cora beamed at him, and then caught his mother's amused expression. Instantly she felt her cheeks going warm. It must be obvious to Mrs. Muller, and to everyone else in the room, that she and Isaac were sweethearts, but to her great relief, no one at the table seemed upset by the idea.

Cora allowed herself to bask in that luxurious sense of acceptance for just a few minutes – in the wonderful assurance that if she joined the church, that *Isaac's* family at least would give her a chance.

In accordance with prior instructions, the children had been silent during dinner, but apparently Caleb had grown tired of keeping big news in. He tapped his spoon on his plate and looked up at his father.

"Daed, when are you going to tell everybody that we're having a new baby?" he asked innocently.

Joseph threw his hands up in the air. "*Now*, I guess, Caleb!" he snorted, and laughed. Adie and Theodor cried out in joy, and Cora noticed that Isaac put on a decent show of surprise as well. When Adie had hugged Katie, and Theodor had slapped Joseph on the back, and congratulations passed all round, Theodor proposed that they open the wine bottle to celebrate.

"Children, go play outside so that the adults can talk," Katie told them. She looked up and made eye contact with Cora.

"Cora, why don't you take Isaac out on the porch, as well. The two of you can talk more comfortably."

Cora silently blessed Katie, and took Isaac's hand. They walked down the front steps of the porch, and around the side of the house to the yard swing. It was early evening, and one sharp star glittered in the pale blue sky.

They sat together in the swing and were silent for awhile. "I'm glad you and your parents came," Cora said at last. "You were right. It *is* better this way."

Isaac smiled. "My parents like you, Cora," he said.

"Oh, Isaac," she sighed, and put her head on his shoulder, "you don't know how relieved I am to hear that. I like them, too. It's so wonderful to know that there are *some* people in this place who don't judge me!"

"My parents would never do that, Cora," he reassured her. "You and my mother are going to be great friends, once you get to know one another. And I don't think people are as set against you as you think. There are plenty of people here who love you."

Cora stirred uncomfortably on his chest. "If you say so!" she replied.

"Well, there's your family, and there's mine," Isaac said softly. "And Mrs. Stoltzfus has been kind to you. That must mean that she likes you."

"You know how to cheer me up, Isaac," she smiled. "You *always* look on the bright side! And yes, Mrs. Stoltzfus has been kind," Cora admitted.

"I'm glad you decided to help her out at the school," he said softly. "I have a feeling you'll be good at teaching."

"I wish *I* felt that way," Cora answered. "The children seem to like me well enough, and I'm finally beginning to be able to answer some of their questions. But Mary Stoltzfus looks at me like she wishes I was a thousand miles away."

Isaac was silent.

"She might be a little jealous, Cora," he said at last. "It can't be easy for her, to have to make room for someone new. It might help, if you kind of – I don't know – tried to get to know her outside of school."

"*Mary Stoltzfus?*" Cora blurted incredulously. "Oh, Isaac, she's the dullest, strangest girl in the world! Whenever I try to talk to her, she just stares at me, and I've never seen her smile, not even once! You might as well ask me to make conversation with a rock!"

"Maybe she hasn't had much practice," Isaac replied gently. "Think about it, anyway. It might help."

"Only *you* could think of something like that, Isaac Muller," Cora told him, smiling. "Because you're a *big, sweet marshmallow.*"

Isaac's eyes widened in astonishment. "*What* did you call me?"

"I said you're a *big, sweet, marshmallow,*" she replied, and kissed him.

When their lips had parted, Isaac took her chin in his hand. "Any chance that a big, sweet marshmallow can get an answer to an important question?" he whispered, and he was no longer smiling.

Cora's smile faded as well. "Oh, Isaac, I – " she began, but was saved unexpectedly by the children, who suddenly came tearing around the side of the house. Cora pulled back instantly, and Isaac turned away and looked down at the ground.

To Cora's relief, the children gave Isaac no more opportunities to ask her difficult questions. They darted back and forth across the lawn, laughing and giggling, until the Mullers appeared on the front porch, and Katie and Joseph followed.

"Well, Isaac, are you coming?" his father called.

Isaac stood up, hat in hand. "Yes, I'll be right there." He looked down at Cora and added, under his breath: "*You know what I was going to say, Cora. Please think about it.*"

Cora looked down, nodded, but dared not reply. She watched as Isaac and the Mullers walked slowly down the front path, still talking to Katie and Joseph, and finally took to the narrow road to their farm, with waves and smiles.

Isaac trailed far behind his parents. When Katie and Joseph had turned to the house, he looked back over his shoulder, still questioning her with his eyes.

CHAPTER TEN

Cora stayed in the swing for a few minutes, listening to the sounds inside and outside the house – Katie calling the children in, the thunder of their feet galloping up the porch steps and into the house, the first soft hum of crickets waking up in the grass, and Katie and Joseph settling into the porch swing.

Eventually, she tired of sitting. As Cora walked across the yard, she could hear their soft voices, discussing baby names.

"What about Rebecca, if it's a girl?" Katie was saying.

"You're hoping for a girl, are you?" Joseph replied, and there was the sound of soft laughter.

"I like Rebecca," she pressed.

"Rebecca is all right with me. But what if it's a boy?"

"What about Jacob?"

"I have a cousin Jacob. Let's think of something else."

Cora climbed the porch steps, and Katie and Joes looked up. "Well, what did *Isaac Muller* have to say?" Katie asked, just a little archly.

Cora smiled. "Nothing new," she replied, and went inside.

And I had nothing new to answer, she thought to herself. She drifted back into the kitchen, going through the motions of helping Emma clean up the dinner dishes, of washing pots and pans and plates, of putting things away.

"Cora!"

Cora looked up. Emma was looking at her in mild exasperation, hands on hips.

"What did I just say?"

Cora smiled crookedly and shook her head. "I'm sorry, Emma. My mind's off somewhere else tonight."

Emma's green eyes held a knowing expression. "I'll bet I can guess *where*, too," she smiled.

Cora rolled up a towel and snapped it at her niece, laughing. She didn't see the point of denying the truth anymore, at least not with Joes' family. If Emma knew, then they *all* knew.

"You're so lucky, Cora. Isaac Muller is the handsomest boy in the county," Emma told her, wiping off a dish. "He's *nice*, too. All the girls in town are crazy about him."

Cora allowed herself a tiny smile, a little nod. Yes, it was true. Isaac had grown into a very handsome fellow, and he didn't have the faintest idea of it. He was also a *truly* good man.

She was very lucky.

But all she said was: "Can you finish up, Emma? There isn't much left. I'm a little tired tonight. I'd like to go to bed early."

"*Sweet dreams*," Emma teased her, giggling.

***

But when she got to her bedroom, and closed the door behind her, Cora didn't feel sleepy. She pulled a chair up to the window facing across the fields to the Muller's farm.

She was thinking about the *ordnung*, and of all the things you were supposed to promise when you joined the church. Obedience to elders, obedience to a husband, living plain, dressing plain, rarely travelling, keeping separate from the world. Never hitting back, even if you were hit *first*.

And all the things about God: believing in God, obeying God, loving God.

Cora propped her elbows on the windowsill, searching her own heart. *Do I believe in God?*

She thought about it for awhile, and had to admit that the answer was: *Yes*.

Do I obey God?

She had to admit, that the answer was usually: *No*. At least if by "obey," you meant obedience to the *ordnung*.

Do I love God?

Cora searched her heart, and the answer was: *I don't know. God, do you love me?*

She looked longingly at the roof of the Muller farmhouse, now only barely visible in the twilight.

Oh God, she prayed, I love Isaac Muller, and I think I want to be his wife. But if I marry Isaac, I'll have to join the church. And then I wouldn't just be giving my heart to him. I'd sort of be giving my heart to You, too, isn't that right?

And we haven't always been on such good terms, You and I. I'm afraid not, anyway. You know how badly I've messed up. I'm sorry, I really am. I wish I could go back and change it all, but I can't!

And now I'm scared. I'm afraid I might mess up again. Everyone knows about what happened with Matt, and now they're watching me, waiting for me to mess up again. But how can I live here all my life, if my husband is the only one who doesn't hate me?

Lord, I hope You don't hate me. If You aren't mad at me,

please show me. And if You want me to marry Isaac, please show me a way that I can fit in here, because right now, I don't see one.

Amen.

She lifted her head. It was dark now, and the little yellow light was burning from one of the Mullers' windows. As always, Cora imagined it as Isaac's bedroom. Was he standing at his window, looking out into the night, too?

Oh, Isaac, she thought, and sagged against the window. I wish you weren't so determined to be Amish. I wish you could be happy somewhere else. Then we wouldn't have these problems. We could run away together, and never look back!

She undressed slowly and sadly, and crawled into the little narrow bed. She lay there for a long time, staring up at the ceiling. *Sweet dreams*, Emma had said. *Well, I wish.*

Cora sighed, turned, and put her hands over her face, until sleep slowly overtook her.

But that night, whether from Emma's blessing or for some other reason, Cora's dreams *were* sweet. She and Isaac were down at the little creek again, sitting on the branch of the oak tree, listening to the soft murmur of the water. She was leaning against his chest, listening to the steady rhythm of his heart.

Neither of them spoke. There was no need to fill the

perfect peace of that place with words: they were comfortable together in silence.

She looked out across the Mullers' green fields, and the road beyond, and the landscape was safe and friendly, a place where she could walk freely with Isaac in the sight of all.

Katie and Joseph called from the house, and came walking down the slope toward them, smiling and laughing. Emma and the boys followed, and then her parents, and then the Mullers, carrying a bottle of wine.

Mrs. Stoltzfus and the children at school appeared, to her great delight, laughing and twirling and playing.

They all threw blankets down on the grass, and brought baskets of food, and ate and drank. And there was no discord, never a word of blame or anger, only harmony.

Only *peace*.

Then Katie reached into her basket and lifted out a baby, a beautiful pink little girl baby with the faintest down of blonde hair.

And Joseph said: "We won't call her Rebecca, after all. We'll call her Dorathea."

Everyone laughed and clapped their hands, and as they did, Isaac put his lips to her ear and whispered: "I have a gift for you, too, Cora. *Look*."

She looked down, and Isaac lifted a blanket to reveal a

baby boy with big, blue eyes. He reached up with a big hand, grabbed her finger, and dimpled in delight.

And even in her sleep, Cora cried out, smiled, and stretched her arms into the air.

CHAPTER ELEVEN

"Cora, I'm so pleased with the way you've taken hold here," Mrs. Stoltzfus smiled. "You have a real way with the children, and you're learning the lessons fast. I knew you'd be good at this, and you are."

Cora looked down at her feet, but could feel herself blushing. It felt *so good* to be praised, for once!

They were talking together in the empty schoolroom as the children played outside for recess. Mary was outside also, supervising them.

"I've really enjoyed it, Mrs. Stoltzfus," she replied softly. "There for a while I didn't think I could do it."

"Please – call me Fannie. You're all grown up now, after all -- a young woman."

Cora felt herself going red. "All right -- F-Fannie." Even though she'd been invited, it felt odd to call her former teacher by her first name.

"Would you like to continue?" Mrs. Stoltzfus asked.

Cora looked up in surprise. "I didn't know you wanted my help *permanently*," she stammered.

"I think you and Mary make a great team," Mrs. Stoltzfus told her confidently. "Mary has the knowledge and experience, and you have the way with children. I think the two of you are better together, than either one alone."

Cora gaped at her. She had always imagined that her job was temporary. The idea of working side-by-side with Mary Stoltzfus, *forever*, was so frankly horrifying that she had to look down quickly to keep Mary's mother from reading that thought right off her face.

Mrs. Stoltzfus' voice softened. "You don't have to give me an answer right away," she said kindly. "But I really hope you give it serious consideration. I think you have a real gift for working with children, Cora. They like you, and it's clear that you like them."

Cora looked up. "Yes, I do," she admitted. "It's *fun* to work with them."

"That's it exactly," Mrs. Stoltzfus replied softly, and it seemed to Cora, a little sadly. "That's your gift, Cora. You have *fun*. And when the children are with you, they have fun, too."

"I'll think about it, Mrs. St – *Fannie*. I promise," Cora told her.

"Good," Mrs. Stoltzfus smiled. "Now, recess is over, and about time! It looks like it's going to rain! Can you ring the bell, Cora, and bring the children in?"

Cora obeyed dutifully, and as she rang the bell, the children came running back into the schoolroom. The seats quickly filled up, and last of all, Mary came in – dour and unsmiling as ever, Cora noticed.

"Mary, turn up the lamps, won't you?" Mrs. Stoltzfus asked. "It's getting dark outside. I'm afraid we may be in for a storm!"

Mary trimmed the kerosene lamps, and turned up the lights. Sure enough, the sky outside became quite dark, and the yellow light of the lamps quickly became the only illumination.

Mrs. Stoltzfus began her lessons, going to this group and that, but a vivid flash of spring lightning, followed by a deep clap of thunder, drowned out the sound of her voice.

She began again, but lightning branched across the sky outside a second time, followed by an even louder crack of thunder.

The younger children put their hands over their ears and looked frightened – including Caleb. Cora smiled, feeling sorry for her little nephew, and moved toward him. Caleb looked as if he needed a little reassurance.

Suddenly there was an electric *crack*, a blinding flash of light, and thunder so loud that it shook the building. Cora closed her eyes for a split-second, but the sound of shattering glass, a *whoosh*, and a terrible scream, caused them to fly open wide.

To her horror, one of the children had knocked a kerosene lamp to the floor, and it had exploded in a ball of fire. And Caleb – *Caleb* was engulfed in flames. He jumped up, screaming and flailing wildly with his arms.

Cora grabbed for him, but he was already on his feet, running crazily for the door. His hair and his clothes were trailing fire. All around them, the children were screaming until a second terrible crack of lightning made them all cower down.

"Caleb, stop!" Cora screamed, and then, when he kept running, she threw herself into the air. She caught his heel and they both slammed to the floor, and as soon as she had him, she clambered up and rolled him under her body over and over, slapping at him with her hands, until the fire was put out.

When she stopped, Caleb lay on the floor beneath her, deathly still. His hair was shriveled and smoldering and he was curled into a fetal position. The sight nearly stopped Cora's heart.

She shook him, searched him over frantically with her fingers. His eyebrows were singed, his hair was burned down to the scalp, his shirt was black and scorched, and he had an ugly red weal across his right ear, his jaw, and one hand.

"Caleb, are you all right?"

He looked up, wild-eyed, and began sobbing.

But to Cora's intense relief, he seemed to have no worse injuries.

She grabbed Caleb and hugged him to her. She became aware that she was crying, and that most of the children were crying, as well. Fannie Stoltzfus was beating the burning kerosene lamp with her cape, and Mary was standing stock-still at the front of the room, paralyzed, her eyes wide and terrified.

"*Auntie, auntie, auntie!*" Caleb was sobbing, and Cora lifted him up in her arms.

Fannie Stoltzfus appeared at Cora's elbow and lifted Caleb's face in her hands. "Poor little man!" she cried in a quavering voice. "Let me look at that face!" She quickly inspected his jaw, neck, and hands. "Yes, he has some burns, but they don't look *very* serious. It could have been much, much worse."

She closed her eyes and let out a long, shuddering sigh. "Cora Lapp, you are a brave young woman," she exclaimed. "If you hadn't gotten to him when you did, I don't like to think what might have happened! Give him to me, and I'll bandage his burns. Then you and I will take him home to his mother. School is over for today!"

Cora followed Fannie Stoltzfus as she sat Caleb down on her desk and opened a first-aid kit. Caleb was still holding tightly to Cora's hand, crying and shivering.

"Oh, auntie's burned, *too!*" he sobbed.

Cora looked down. It was only then that she realized that her hair had come undone, and that bits of it were drifting oddly around her face. One of her sleeves was nearly burned off, and the whole front of her dress was black and scorched. She became aware of a dull pain in her right hand.

"Good heavens, Cora -- you need attention, too!" Fannie Stoltzfus exclaimed.

She got a basin of cool water and gently washed Caleb and Cora's wounds, applied burn ointment, then bandaged them loosely. By this time, Caleb had stopped crying, but he still clung to Cora's hand.

"Mary, stay with the children until the storm is over, and then send them home," Mrs. Stoltzfus commanded. "I'm driving Cora and Caleb home."

She tried to pick Caleb up into her arms, but he wouldn't be satisfied with anyone but Cora. So Cora picked him up and carried him to Mrs. Stoltzfus' buggy.

All during the long drive home, Caleb sat shivering in Cora's lap with his thumb stuck in his mouth. The rain was still pelting down. Cora held him close, murmuring comfort in his ear, but in spite of the burn cream her shoulder and hand had begun to throb, and she was getting a splitting headache behind her eyes.

By the time they reached Joseph's house, Cora's legs and arms had begun to tremble. When they stopped, she had to let Fannie Stoltzfus take Caleb, because she didn't know if she could carry him inside.

The sound of the buggy pulling up had drawn Emma out onto the porch, but the sight of Caleb's singed head brought her running out to meet them.

"Emma, go get your mother," Mrs. Stoltzfus told her. "Caleb is all right, but there's been an accident at school."

Emma turned on her heel and ran inside. Mrs. Stoltzfus had barely climbed out of the buggy, and taken Caleb up into her arms, when Katie burst out of the house and came running toward them.

But to Cora's dismay, when she was halfway there, Katie jerked to an abrupt stop. She stared at Caleb's bald, singed head, his bandaged jaw, and his blackened clothes, and such a look of horror filled her eyes that even Fannie Stoltzfus seemed taken back.

"*Katie,*" she began gently, "*Caleb is all right,* but there's been an accident at school. A kerosene lamp caught fire –"

Katie put a hand up to her mouth and shook her head violently. A strangled, animal scream burst from her throat, and she fled back into the house without another word.

CHAPTER TWELVE

"What's wrong with Mamm?" Caleb wailed.

They were all staring at the house, speechless.

Mrs. Stoltzfus recovered first. "Your mamm will be all right, Caleb," she told him. "Let's get you inside."

But to Emma, who was still standing on the porch, she said: "*Go get your father, now.*"

Cora followed them inside the house, feeling chilled and sick. Fannie Stoltzfus put Caleb down on the couch and bundled him up in blankets.

"Cora, it might help to --" She turned, and her voice trailed off.

"On second thought, you sit down, dear," she amended. "I'll see if I can find something for you and Caleb in the kitchen."

Mrs. Stoltzfus rummaged in the pantry, and soon she returned with hot coffee and biscuits for Cora, and milk and cookies for Caleb. Cora took the coffee gratefully. The warmth was good. She still felt weak and cold and not quite right, somehow.

Cora looked up at the stairs as she drank, wondering uneasily why Katie had run to hide, when Caleb was hurt and needed her. It was plain that something was *very* wrong. She was wondering if she should try to go upstairs and comfort her, when Joseph burst into the living room.

"*Daed, Daed!*" Caleb shrieked.

Joseph caught Caleb up in his arms, kissed him over and over, and then held him close. When he pulled back to look at his son, Cora noticed that his eyes were wet.

"Are you all right, Caleb?" he cried.

Caleb nodded wordlessly.

Mrs. Stoltzfus explained, "A lamp exploded at school, and Caleb got burned, but Cora got to him and put out the fire before it could hurt him badly."

Joseph looked down at Cora, tried to say something, and couldn't. He put his hand on her head. Then he asked thickly: "*Where's Katie?*"

"She ran upstairs, Joes," Cora told him quietly.

His eyes wandered to the stairs. "Go and change, sprout,"

he told her. "I'll tend to Caleb."

Then he turned to Mrs. Stoltzfus. "Thank you, Fannie," he said quietly. "Thank you for bringing them home."

"I can stay, if you like," she offered, but Joseph shook his head. "You've done so much already," he told her. "We'll be all right."

Mrs. Stoltzfus came to Caleb and put a hand to his cheek. "You're going to be okay now," she assured him. Then she turned to Cora. "Rest up, Cora. I don't expect to see you at school for a few days at least."

Cora nodded gratefully. "Thank you, Fannie."

***

Mrs. Stoltzfus left, and no sooner had the door closed behind her, than Joseph whisked Caleb upstairs. Cora found herself sitting in the living room, alone except for Emma.

"Your *hair*, Cora," Emma said suddenly.

Cora put a hand to her head. To her dismay, when she pulled it back, some of her hair came back with it.

"Oh, *Cora*," Emma wailed softly. "Your beautiful hair – it's singed off! You're going to have to cut it *short!*"

Cora felt her lip beginning to tremble. And since she didn't care to let Emma see her blubber like a baby, she rose and announced that she was going to go bathe, and change her clothes.

She gathered her skirts and walked out slowly, being careful to use the back stairs. Since her bedroom was nearest the stairs, the last on the upper hall, using this route would keep her farthest from Katie and Joes, and at the moment, Cora was anxious to give them their privacy.

She slipped into the upstairs bathroom and closed the door. She took a deep breath, lifted her shoulders, and took a look at herself in the mirror.

"Oh!"

Cora clapped a hand to her mouth. All the hair on the right side of her head had been singed off just under her ear. Wisps of burned hair floated around her face in uneven layers, and even around the back of her head, it was ragged and damaged.

To her relief, her face had been unharmed, but her right shoulder and hand were very sore under their bandages. She removed them gingerly, inspecting the burns. Her smooth white shoulder was now a red, ugly, blistered mess. The fingers of her right hand were also swollen, and so sore that she doubted she'd be able to use them properly for at least a week, and maybe more.

She closed her eyes and leaned against the sink. Yes, she told herself, she looked awful, and felt sick and weak, but *Caleb was safe*, and that was all that mattered.

Cora looked at herself again in the mirror. Emma was

right, she was going to have to cut off her hair. There was no other way.

She pinched her lips into a straight line, telling herself that cutting her hair wasn't such a big deal – English girls did it all the time, and she had even toyed with the idea herself once.

So she opened a drawer and yanked out a pair of shears. She looked at herself in the mirror, breathing deeply and thinking, *I can do this.*

Then, before she had a chance to change her mind, she quickly chopped off all her hair in a straight, severe line just under her ears.

Cora glared at herself defiantly in the mirror. *There.*

She looked ridiculous now, just like a boy, but everyone else was *just going to have to like it.* She gathered up the silken pile of her soft blonde hair, and threw it into the waste basket.

Then she turned on the shower water, being careful to keep it on the cool side of lukewarm, and gently washed the smell of smoke off of her hair and body.

When she had finished, she replaced her bandages, wrapped herself in a robe and crept back to her own bedroom. She tossed the burned clothes away and put on her blue Sunday dress.

The house was unusually quiet, and though she tried not to,

she couldn't help hearing voices from further down the hall. Joseph was apparently with Katie now, because she could hear his low voice, murmuring soothing, unintelligible words.

And though she wished she didn't, she also heard Katie: the walls of the farmhouse couldn't completely blot out the sound of her sobs. Occasionally Katie's voice rose in a crescendo of anguish, and once Cora clearly heard her shriek: *gone, gone, gone*!

The pain in that sound wrung Cora's heart, and it also frightened her. Katie had always been so strong, but now she seemed to be almost *sick*.

And Joes depended on Katie – *a lot*.

Maybe *she* could help him, while Katie was feeling unwell.

She crept soundlessly out of her room, and down the hall just as far as the boys' bedroom. Caleb was lying in his little bed, fast asleep, worn out by his ordeal. An empty cup and a freshly eaten apple core lay on the table beside his bed, and Cora crept in and removed them.

His baby face looked swollen, and his scalp was bare and scorched, but he was still Joes' adorable six-year-old, and Cora felt something almost maternal stirring in her as she watched him sleep. She had to repress a shudder, when she remembered how close they had all come to losing him.

A small, quiet thought came to her then: *Thank you, God, that we didn't.*

Then she withdrew, and returned to the kitchen the way she had come.

CHAPTER THIRTEEN

When Cora walked back into the kitchen, the boys had returned from the fields and were sitting at the table, looking worried and glum. They glanced up at her, and then froze.

"*Yes*, I cut my hair," she told them tartly. "Go ahead and stare at it!"

The boys looked down, and then at each other.

"It looks – it looks kind of cool," Jeremiah shrugged.

"Yeah. Kind of English," Hezekiah mumbled. "But don't tell *Daed* I said it."

Cora stared at them in disbelief, but they seemed to be sincere. She tossed her head, shrugged.

"Katie isn't feeling well," she told them, "so we're on our own tonight. Emma and I will get something started, while you two wash up. Caleb's asleep upstairs, so be quiet!"

The boys rose and went upstairs, and Cora and Emma were just beginning to prepare for dinner, when there was a soft knock at the door.

"Come in," Cora called.

News in the community travelled fast, and word of the day's events had already reached the Mullers. Isaac and Adie Muller stood in the living room, and when their eyes found Cora, they widened.

Cora was suddenly aware that she had never felt so ugly, or so embarrassed, in her entire life. She looked down at the floor to avoid meeting their eyes. *They were staring at her hair.*

Mrs. Muller stepped forward. "I brought some food," she said, and placed a large basket on the kitchen table. "We won't stay, you are tired. But we heard what happened and wanted to help. How is Caleb?"

"He has a few burns, but he's all right, thank you for asking," Cora murmured politely. "It was kind of you to think of us."

"Good, very good! I'm glad to hear that he's all right, poor thing! And *you*, Cora. Well, I'll be going, you will want to rest. Please give Joseph and Katie our love."

She leaned forward unexpectedly, and gave Cora a quick peck on the cheek. Cora went red to the ears and mumbled:

"I will, thank you, Mrs. Muller."

Mrs. Muller smiled and departed, but Isaac didn't follow her. He was looking at Cora's bandaged hand.

"Are you all right, Cora?" he asked softly.

Perversely, his forbearance made her want to scream.

"Oh, go ahead and say it, Isaac Muller!" she burst out. *"What did you do to your hair?* Well, I chopped it off because most of it was *burned* off and I looked like a circus monkey! And I'm wearing my Sunday dress because my everyday is burned black and stinks of smoke! And, and," her voice cracked, "I've never been so scared in my *life* and I'm *tired* and *sick* and I wish I could – "

But she didn't get to finish, because Isaac simply put his arms around her and pulled her into his chest, where she began to cry.

He opened the door and they went outside and sat down on the porch, where she continued to cry on his chest, and he murmured comforting words into her ear that mostly didn't make any sense: something about a soft bird, and a kitten, and over and over again, *my brave girl.*

Then he inspected the bandage on her hand, and lifted it up and kissed it. By this time, Cora's sobs had subsided to occasional hiccups, and Isaac considered that those needed mending, too. Soon she was wrapped in Isaac's arms, and he was kissing her cheeks, her nose, her eyelids. His hands moved to her hair, caressing her smooth cap of blonde silk.

He pulled back long enough to tell her gravely: "I like it."

Cora looked up at him and cried again. "Oh, Isaac, it's hideous," she sobbed, "and only you would be so kind. You're so..." she began, but the touch of his lips on hers put an end to further talking.

Cora wound her arms around him and abandoned herself to the touch of his lips, to the feel of her fingers in his hair, to the way his skin smelled and tasted: clean and sweet and a tiny bit salty, smooth and rough at the same time, and always so comforting. She stopped kissing him and pressed her cheek to his chest, listening to his heart just as she had done in her lovely dream.

Only this time, its beat was not steady. It was thumping under her jaw like a bass drum, and she drank up that sound like wine. Nothing, *nothing* was better in life than this: to lie in Isaac Muller's arms and listen to the beating of his heart. Isaac was better for her than any doctor or medicine, and nothing soothed her like his touch, and the sound of his voice.

"I wish I'd been there today, Cora," he murmured. "I can't stand the thought of you being hurt. I'm so grateful to God that you're all right!"

He pulled her closer. "I wish we were married," he whispered. "I could take you home with me, and hold you in my arms all night."

Cora looked up at him, put her hand to his cheek. "Oh, Isaac, I'd never be afraid of anything *then*," she told him.

He kissed her, and a second time, and then told her: "I'll stay here tonight, if you want. I'll sleep on the swing, if I have to. But I want to be here, close to you."

Cora looked at him and shook her head. "You wouldn't *fit* on the swing, Isaac!" she smiled. "But you're the sweetest man in the world, and I – I *love* you!"

He suddenly fell quiet, and *so* quiet that it was like he was holding his breath. At first Cora didn't understand why, but then she remembered – it was the first time she'd actually told Isaac Muller, in so many words, that she *loved* him.

She'd known it herself for a long time, of course; Isaac *had* to know it by now; everyone else in town probably knew it.

But now it was *official*.

She bit her lip, because she knew what was coming next: Isaac was going to ask her to marry him, and she *still* didn't have an answer.

But to her relief, he didn't get the chance that afternoon. The door opened. Joes had finally come out to look for her.

Cora half-expected Isaac to jump up at the sight of Joes, but he held her as tight as ever, even when Joseph came close.

Then she was afraid that Joes was going to get mad, like he had when he'd caught Isaac kissing her in the buggy that day.

But she needn't have worried. Joes simply put out his hand, and pulled her up out of Isaac's embrace, and into his own.

He hugged her tight, and Cora frowned: she could feel the exhaustion in his body.

"I didn't get a chance to tell you before, sprout," he said quietly. "But *thank you, thank you, thank you.* We can *never* repay you."

Cora felt tears prick her eyelids, and she gave him a quick peck on the cheek. "You don't have to thank me, Joes," she told him.

"You saved my life today. But I still need your help, Cora," he sighed. "I need for you to take the children to Mamm and Daed's tomorrow. Katie is having a very hard time. The sight of Caleb's burns was a terrible shock to her. It brought back bad memories from when she lost her first son. She's going to need a few days of rest – maybe more."

"Oh, Joes, is she going to be all right?" Cora cried softly.

"I'm sure she will," he replied, in a cracking voice. "But I'm going to call a doctor."

"Oh, of course I'll help you, Joes," Cora promised, hugging him, "Anything! You know how I love Katie. But I want to stay, even if the children go. You're going to need someone to help you."

"We'll talk about that later, sprout," he replied gently. "You've done more than enough for one day. Come inside and go to bed. We've all been through the wringer today, and you especially."

He looked down at Isaac.

"Isaac, please thank your parents for us. It was very kind of them to bring food. I'm sorry I wasn't there when you and your mother arrived."

"Is there anything I can do?" Isaac asked.

"Not now, but thank you, son."

Isaac stood up slowly. "I'll be going," he said, looking at Cora. "If you need anything, you only need to ask, and I'll be here." He suddenly remembered Joseph's sensibilities, and added: "...If that's all right with you, Mr. Lapp."

Joseph looked at him and sighed, "Isaac, as far as I'm concerned, you can come to see Cora here, as often as you like."

Cora's face brightened, and she reached out and squeezed Isaac's hand.

"As long as you do it in the *daytime*," Joseph finished significantly, and then took Cora's arm, and pulled her back inside.

"Thank you, Mr. Lapp," Isaac replied, in a tone that communicated gratitude -- and more than a little chagrin.

CHAPTER FOURTEEN

The next morning, Cora helped all the children pack their things, and bundled them into Joseph's buggy for a trip to their grandparents. Once they were all in, she came back inside for one last word with Joes.

"We're off," she told him. "I'll be back as soon as they get settled in." She glanced up at the stairs. "How's Katie this morning?"

Joes looked down at the floor and pinched his lips together. "Crying," he replied tersely. "I can't get her to eat. I've called her parents, and they're on the way over."

"Oh, *Joes*," Cora murmured.

He lifted his chin, looked off towards the kitchen. "I called Mamm and Daed, too. They're expecting you. You should stay with them, you know, once you get there."

"I'm coming back this afternoon," Cora replied. "You'll

need someone to cook and help with the house."

"Thank you, Cora." Joseph patted her shoulder, but didn't meet her eyes.

They walked out to the buggy in silence. In spite of the mild weather, Caleb was bundled up to the ears in a soft blanket and was sitting in Emma's lap.

Joseph leaned in and gave his son a tender kiss. "You be good for Dawdy and Mammi, Caleb," he murmured. "I'll be there tonight."

Cora climbed up into the driver's seat, and with a wave, she shook the reins. As the buggy moved off, she looked back over her shoulder. Joes was standing in the middle of the road with his hand still raised, and his mouth was pulled down in an expression of dismay that reminded her almost of Caleb.

***

The weather was fine and clear, and if they had all been less worried, it might have been a pleasant ride. Caleb had been given pain medication, and the slow swaying of the buggy soon lulled him to sleep. Emma and the boys were subdued, looking out across the green landscape in brooding silence.

Cora pretended cheerfulness that she was far from feeling, sometimes even humming or singing a bit, in an attempt to lighten the mood.

But all the time she was thinking about Katie, and wondering just *how* bad she was. Cora hardly needed to have heard Katie crying to know that she was in crisis. The bare fact that she had not yet rushed to Caleb was enough to show that she must be in a terrible way: nothing short of an illness could have kept her from him.

Cora was beginning to fear that the sight of Caleb's burns had pushed Katie into some kind of serious emotional breakdown, and to judge by the silence in the buggy, it was a fear the others shared.

But Cora hummed and sang to herself the whole way, hoping that the old saying was true: *fake it until you make it.*

***

The Lapp farmhouse was one of the oldest in the county, and very large: the effect from afar was that it was more of a compound than a single dwelling, since many of Cora's older brothers had built on, or built nearby. As Joseph had promised, they were expected: as their buggy topped the last rise, Cora was heartened to see that there were many other buggies gathered in her parents' yard. She shook the reins, and the horse quickened its pace.

As they got nearer, some of her younger nieces and nephews came running out to meet them, and one or two jumped into the back seat, laughing and giggling.

The boys had already begun to perk up a bit, and for her

part, the sight of her brothers standing out in the front yard, and the children running to meet them, and her mamm and daed standing on the porch, sent a wave of relief coursing through Cora's heart. For the last 24 hours she had felt almost like the sole – and very inadequate -- caretaker for the children. Now, she was able to deliver them to *much* more capable hands.

She pulled the buggy right up into the front yard of her parents' house, and in the babel of voices that followed, Cora could hear her mother crying, "*Cora! Cora!*"

She jumped down from the buggy and went straight to her arms.

Her mamm folded her close, and put her soft hands around Cora's face. "We're glad you're back, Cora, our brave girl," she cried, kissing her cheek. "Joseph told us what happened, how you saved Caleb's life! The whole town is talking."

Cora's relief faded. "They *are?*" she stammered.

Her mother smiled. "Yes! They are all saying what a brave girl you are, and how smart. *We* won't argue!"

Cora looked back toward the buggy, and saw that it had been swarmed by the children. Their mothers had to come and sweep them back, so that they could help Emma and Caleb out.

But her daed couldn't wait: he waded in, lifted Caleb right out of Emma's arms, and carried him straight inside, followed by her brothers and sisters, and a good many of the children. Both of Cora's parents had always doted on Caleb, and it was clear to her that he was going to spend his time here being spoiled to death by Dawdy and Mammi and a lot of other relatives, as well. Some of her cousins were already arm in arm with Emma, and the boys had disappeared.

"Come inside, Cora," her mother urged her, "We have lunch all laid out. You can unpack your things after you eat."

"I'll have a bite, mamm, but I'm going right back," Cora told her. "I promised Joes that I'd stay with him for a while longer to help with Katie."

Her mother's face fell, but she nodded. "You'll be a great help to him, Cora," she replied. "I won't be selfish. But we've missed you." She ran her fingers mournfully over Cora's chopped-off hair, and then noticed her bandaged hand.

"You must let me look after you, at least for a little while," Cora's mother told her -- and Cora nodded. She liked to think of herself as an adult, but after the time she'd had, Cora told herself, a little TLC from her mother would still be very welcome.

***

Her mother led her to the dining room, and Cora sat down at her parent's huge table with all of her relatives. It was a rare pleasure for Cora: an abundant, delicious meal that *she* had no hand in preparing.

Conversation was lively, and Cora was surprised by how often her brothers and sisters and in-laws commented, during the meal, of how many other people had asked after Caleb, *and* her, and had praised her quick thinking.

"Fannie Stoltzfus said that you were the only one who didn't panic," Cora's niece said shyly.

"People in town are saying that you're a *hero*, Cora," one of her little cousins giggled, only to have her father rebuke her with a stern, "Enough of that talk, child – you shouldn't tempt another to vanity. *Hochmut!*"

Cora put a spoonful of lima beans into her mouth, but raised her eyebrows just a little, all the same.

After lunch was over, Cora stayed long enough to let her mother dress her burns, put fresh bandages on, load her down with food, and give her a little travelling bag full of clothes. But she had promised Joes that she'd come right back, and pressed her mother to let her go.

Her mother sighed, and caressed her hair. "You're doing right to help your brother, and Katie," she told her, "but remember, Cora, the outcome is in the hands of God. There is only so much that any of us can do. We must trust Him."

Cora nodded silently, but frowned.

She was wondering, uneasily, if maybe her mamm knew something that *she* didn't.

CHAPTER FIFTEEN

Cora took the buggy back the way she had come. The day had blossomed mild and fair, and everywhere she looked, there were fields fragrant with the new green of spring.

But neither the warm welcome she had just received, nor the beautiful day, was able to calm her worry. She flicked the horse's ears, urging it to quicken its pace. For the first time since she had returned, she wished she had a car, so she could speed along these sleepy roads as fast as her worried imagination.

By the time Cora got back to Joes' house, there was another buggy in the yard, one that she recognized as belonging to the Fishers, Katie's parents.

When she entered the house, she found John Fisher sitting in Joes' overstuffed chair. He was a portly, gray-haired man with sad brown eyes. He looked up at her silently.

"I'm Cora, Joseph's sister," Cora said. "You're Katie's

daed, aren't you?"

He looked at her, nodded.

And because she could think of nothing else to say, she added: "Would you like something to eat, Mr. Fisher?"

He shook his head, and looked down at the floor.

"Well, I'm going to make you something anyway," Cora told him. "Do you like coffee or tea?"

A flicker of surprise crossed his face. "Coffee."

Well, at least he perked up a little, Cora thought, and went to make some.

"Decaf," he added suddenly, and Cora smiled.

As she brewed the coffee, and made sandwiches and potato salad, Cora could hear muffled voices from upstairs. Katie's agitated voice, on and off, and another female voice, a voice that was always low and calm.

To Cora's relief, there were no more sobbing sounds.

Joseph came downstairs just as she had finished the coffee, and he grabbed a cup gratefully.

"How is Katie doing?" Mr. Fisher asked.

"Better," Joseph told him. "She took a little juice and toast this morning. The doctor is coming by later to look at her."

Mr. Fisher nodded, and sipped his coffee silently.

***

Cora passed out the sandwiches and potato salad, and told Joes how the children, and Caleb especially, had been received at home as if they'd just returned from Siberia, and that they were likely to be spoiled beyond recognition by the time they got back.

The flicker of relief on Joes' face was comforting. He looked worn, sick with worry, and Cora wished that she could do more to help him than just making sandwiches and small talk.

A little after noon, the doctor arrived, a graying, middle-aged man with glasses and a beard. Joes and Mr. Fisher welcomed him heartily and ushered him upstairs at once.

The house became very quiet -- unnaturally quiet, Cora thought, for the number of people in it. She tried to distract herself with busy work as the time passed. She could hear the doctor's deep voice occasionally, apparently asking questions, and Joes or Mrs. Fisher replying. Though she strained her ears for the sound, Cora couldn't make out Katie's voice. Was that good or bad?

After a half hour had passed, the men came walking noisily down the stairs. The doctor was saying, "I'll call them and make an appointment for you sometime next week. You have my number. You can call me on Monday and I'll tell you what I was able to work out."

Joes gripped the doctor's hand. "Thank you, doctor. I can't tell you how much I appreciate your help."

The two of them walked him out to his car, and after a few more farewells, saw him off.

Cora waited for them, twisting a dish cloth between her fingers.

When Joseph walked in, she pounced on him. "Well, Joes, *what did he say?*"

Joseph sank down on the sofa. "He said that he thinks Katie is suffering from something called post traumatic stress," he replied wearily. "He says that when something very bad happens to a person, sometimes the pain can come back to hurt them, even years later. He said that he thinks that when Katie saw Caleb's burns, it reminded her of losing her first son, Peder, and those bad feelings came back in a powerful way."

"Is she going to be all right, Joes?" Cora asked softly.

Joseph pulled his hands over his face. "He says he thinks so, but she's going to need counseling. Maybe for a long time. He wants us to take her to a specialist."

Cora digested this in silence. Then she looked up.

"Can I see her, Joes?"

He looked at her sadly. "Not yet, sprout. I don't think she's ready for that. But she will be soon, God willing."

Mr. Fisher had returned to the overstuffed chair, and stirred uncomfortably. "I'm worried that Katie hasn't been eating," he said in a low voice. "She needs to build up her strength to get better. It's not good for the baby, either."

"Well, I can send up something for her and Mrs. Fisher to eat," Cora suggested. "Mamm sent three jars of her apple butter and biscuits, plus smoked ham and sweet potato casserole. No one I ever knew could resist them."

Mr. Fisher looked at her. "Katie loves apple butter," he nodded. "*And* ham. Yes, send that up. She might take some of that."

Cora moved to do it, but to her surprise, Katie's father motioned to her to sit down. "Wait. Let's pray together first."

Although she was glad to pray for Katie, *public* prayer always made Cora feel faintly embarrassed. She looked over at Joes, but he nodded and closed his eyes. Cora stifled a sigh and sank down into a chair.

John Fisher bowed his head and began to pray in a low voice.

"Oh Lord, we come to You to ask You to heal our Katze. Please comfort her, Lord, and take away the bad memories that are hurting her. Please bring back her appetite, Lord, so she will eat and become stronger.

"Please bless Joseph, and give him comfort and strength. Please take away any fear or worry from him, and from all of us. Help us to trust you.

"Thank you for the doctor, for his wisdom and skill. Please give all Katze's doctors wisdom to know what to do, so they will give good advice.

"And thank you for Cora, and her helping hands to cook and drive and be an encouragement. Thank you for her courage, and that Caleb is still with his family."

Cora frowned and stirred in her chair, but kept her eyes closed.

"Lord, our eyes are on You. Help us to accept whatever You have for Katze, and for us. We know that You are loving and kind, and we will trust You.

"Amen."

Cora opened her eyes and glanced at Joseph. He wiped his nose and nodded.

"Come up with me, John," he mumbled. "She'll want to see you."

The two of them climbed the stairs, leaving Cora to return to her task, and to wish that she could follow.

But as she worked, Mr. Fisher's prayer echoed in her mind. She had heard many people pray, but John Fisher talked to God as if God was a personal friend. Cora had never thought of God in that way, and she wondered how Mr. Fisher had come to feel so comfortable with Him.

Then too, he had mentioned her by name, and that had startled her. Cora had never heard anyone outside her own family *thank God* for her.

She shook her head, perplexed, and busied herself making plates.

CHAPTER SIXTEEN

John and Mary Fisher stayed with them for several days. Cora fixed up the boys' bedroom for them, cooked lots of meals, and did her best to cheer Joes up.

To her relief, Joes was looking better day by day, because Katie was slowly improving. The drawn, haggard look was fading from his eyes, and once he actually *smiled*.

After a few days, Joseph came to her as she was peeling potatoes in the kitchen, and put his hand on her arm.

"Come upstairs," he said softly. "Katie wants to see you."

Cora smiled, dropped her peeler, and fairly ran up the stairs after him.

Joseph knocked softly on the door, and opened it gently. Cora peeked around his shoulder, and saw Mary Fisher sitting beside Katie's bed, and Katie sitting up, with the remnants of a half-eaten breakfast on a tray.

Katie's hair, usually so neatly pinned, was tumbled wildly around her shoulders. Cora thought that it was strange to see her in a flannel nightgown, instead of her immaculately starched lavender dress.

Cora felt a strange mixture of joy and grief. Joy, because Katie was sitting up, eating her meals, and looking calm: grief, because she was still a shadow of her former beautiful self. Her face was pale and thin, and there were dark circles under her big eyes.

But when she looked up, Cora put on her brightest, most cheerful smile.

"*Oh, Cora*," Katie murmured, opening her arms. Cora went into them without hesitation, and hugged Katie close.

"Darling, I don't know how to thank you," Katie whispered tremulously. "*You saved our Caleb!*"

Cora laughed softly. "You don't have to thank me, Katie," she assured her. "And Caleb is more than fine now, he's a little strutting rooster. I took him to his Dawdy and Mammi, and all of his aunts and uncles, and they dote on him something crazy. If he was any more spoiled, he'd turn English!"

Mrs. Fisher smiled and looked down at her lap, but Katie's nervous fingers plucked at Cora's sleeves. "Oh, Caleb -- how I *miss* him! And Emma, and the boys!" she murmured. She looked up at her husband. "Joseph, *when* are you going to let them come back?"

"Not long now," he promised. "The doctor wants to see you first, remember?"

"Oh, that doctor," she fretted. "What does he know about being a *mother*? The children will be better for me than all the talk in the world."

"I don't doubt it, but we have to do what he says," Joseph replied gently.

Katie turned to Cora with the ghost of a smile. "You see how he bullies me," she told her.

"Don't feel special," Cora retorted, and kissed her cheek. "He's been doing that to me for years." She turned to wink at Joes, and he motioned to her faintly.

Cora turned back to Katie and hugged her. "I won't tire you out," she told her. "But it does my heart good to see you doing so well. You'll be your old self in no time."

Katie returned her embrace, and the two of them parted reluctantly.

***

When Cora and Joes had gone back downstairs, he sat her down on the couch and put his hands on hers. She frowned a little, wondering what was coming *this* time.

"Sprout, I want you to go back to work. You've been a

tremendous help to us, but I can't let you put your own life on hold forever. It isn't fair to you."

Cora put her hands on her hips -- surprised, and none too pleased. "Well, who's going to cook for you, Joes?" she demanded. "You'd be helpless!"

Joseph raised his eyebrows. "You might not believe it, but *I can cook for myself,*" he told her wryly.

"The Fishers..." she began, but he cut her off.

"John and Mary are going home in a few days," he told her gently, "and I want you to go home, too. You need to rest. When the children come back, Emma can cook until Katie is ready to start doing things around the house."

Cora digested this. She looked at Joes, assessing him. The expression on his face told her that he was dead serious.

She sighed. "I'm happy to stay, Joes," she told him.

He looked at her with affection in his eyes. "I know, sprout. You've been really generous. I can't tell you how much you've helped us. But we'll be all right now. Go home -- and be seventeen again." He leaned forward, and kissed her on the brow.

***

That evening after dinner Cora went out onto the porch and sat in the swing, pushing it lazily back and forth with a bare foot. The night was soft and warm, and fireflies rose up from the grass like wandering stars.

Cora looked down the road toward the Mullers', wishing that Isaac would appear in the blue dusk and come and sit down beside her, but the road was empty.

Now that it came to it, she didn't want to leave at all. In spite of her parents' love, and the warmth of her family, these soft, green hills had come to feel more like home.

In spite of everything that had happened, she had been happier here than anywhere else. And now that it was time to go home, she felt a little lost and lonely.

She looked up at the sky. The evening star winked in the blue. Something about the calm, peaceful night, and the humming crickets, and the stars appearing one by one, somehow reminded Cora of Mr. Fisher, and his odd prayer.

The one that made God sound like He wasn't mad.

Like He was a *friend*.

How do you get to know God like that, she wondered, not just hearing about him from someone else, but knowing Him for yourself?

She pushed the swing back and forth.

Talking to Him, maybe. That would make sense, anyway: it was how you got to know everyone else.

Cora looked up at the sky, and prayed: God, I'd like to know you like Mr. Fisher knows you. Or at least, I'd like to think You're not mad at me.

I'd like to make peace with You. I'd like to be friends, Lord Jesus. Is that all right with You?

I know I've done some stupid things, Lord. I messed up really bad, and I'm sorry about that. Please forgive me.

She looked down, bit her lip.

Help me to do things that keep us friends, Lord. And please -- help me not to mess up again.

She ended her prayer, and then searched her heart, but there was no feeling of supernatural change, no sudden revelation. The crickets continued to hum softly in the fields, and the fireflies danced.

The only thing different, was that the old feeling that God was *angry*, had gone away.

And after thinking about it, Cora decided -- that was *enough for her*.

CHAPTER SEVENTEEN

The next morning was a cool, foggy spring dawn, with everything shrouded in gray mist and the fresh scent of dew.

It should have been a pleasant morning for a drive, but Cora hunched in the front seat of Joe's buggy, trying not to pout.

The few bags she had were lying on the back seat where she had thrown them. She sat there with her arms crossed, waiting for Joes to come out of the house.

In her mind, Cora knew that Joes was sending her away out of kindness, that he was thinking of her, and not of his own convenience. It was a sweet and unselfish gesture. It would be much easier for him if she *stayed*, and they both knew it.

But in Cora's heart, the separation felt like a *banishment*.

She had gotten used to the children. She adored Katie, and

in spite of his tedious old-fashioned ideas, she doted on Joes.

To add to her unhappiness, Isaac hadn't come to see her in days, and she missed him, and was beginning to be a little worried that something might be wrong, but she didn't have the nerve to go over to the Mullers' and ask.

This was not Joes' fault, but it would be easier for her to find out about Isaac if she was *here*, instead of *clear across the county*.

The thought suddenly came to her that maybe she could leave Isaac a note, and send it to him by Joes. Joes might not like that, but he'd become a lot more tolerant of her meetings with Isaac lately, and he might agree. She also knew that whatever Joes thought, he would respect their privacy.

She grabbed for her travel bag, and pulled out a little prayer book that her mother had put into it. She tore out a page and fished out a pencil.

Loneliness and longing for Isaac welled up in her heart. How she missed Isaac – and how she hated to go away from him!

Dear Isaac, she wrote. Then she crossed that out and began again.

Isaac my love, she amended, and crossed that out, too.

She finally settled on: My darling Isaac, Joes is sending me back home. My parents won't be as understanding as Joes and

Katie, but I can't stand the thought of not seeing you. I wish we could be together on the porch swing. I miss you so much, I dream of you at night.

She put the pencil in her mouth and read it over, and added, *I dream of kissing your sweet lips.*

She dimpled, thinking of them, and went on: Meet me Sunday week at the sing. Please come. I can't wait to see you again. I am never happier than when I am with you.

Love always,

Cora.

XXOO

She read the note back, considered it perfect, and folded it carefully into a tiny triangle. It was by far the warmest letter that she had ever sent to Isaac, but it conveyed her feelings perfectly and was *sure* to bring him to the sing.

When Joes finally came out to the buggy, Cora was so well pleased with her handiwork that she forgot all about being hurt with him. She wrapped her arms around his neck, and kissed him, and asked him sweetly if he would pass along a message to Isaac for her, since she hadn't had the chance to tell him that she was going home again.

Even with all his preoccupations, her request sparked a suspicious glint in Joseph's eye, but he took the tiny triangle in his hand.

"You aren't *toying* with that boy, are you, sprout?" he asked.

Cora pulled back, genuinely stung. "What a *terrible* thing to say, Joes!" she cried. "You know how I feel about Isaac!"

Joes eyed her uneasily. "Yes -- he's a big, sweet marshmallow," he mumbled, and shook his head.

***

When they finally got to the Lapp farmhouse, the family hailed them as warmly as before. Their parents came out in the yard to meet them, and Joseph's children ran out to hang on his neck, and to hug her.

Their father carried Caleb out onto the porch, and even in the space of a few days, Caleb looked so much better, and so much more pleased with himself and life in general, that a week of stress seemed to lift off Joseph's shoulders. He took Caleb in his arms and kissed him, and laughed, and bounced him in his arms.

Cora watched this happy scene with wistful love, because Joes had come not just to take her home, but to take his children *back*. She realized, with a pang, that her afternoon would seem lonely and quiet after they had gone, no matter how many other loved ones surrounded her. And she missed Isaac with almost physical pain.

To her relief, Joseph was pulled into the house, and they all sat down to lunch. The family kept him for the better part of the afternoon: laughing, talking, getting news about Katie, and giving news of the children. There wasn't much to tell, Cora saw, except that they had eaten too much and been thoroughly and delightfully spoiled.

Joes seemed to revive with the family all around him, she noticed. Her other brothers joked with him as much as they dared, and Cora's older sisters fed him all his favorite treats, and played with the children, and loaded him down with little gifts for Katie: a knitted bed jacket, more apple butter, a book of puzzles.

For her part, Cora picked at her food, and was glad that for once her mamm didn't seem to notice. She didn't feel much like eating.

After dinner was over, and they had talked for a long while, Joseph hugged his parents and his brothers and sisters, and gathered the children.

Cora sat glumly in the corner, absently poking her fried chicken with a fork, and thinking that Joes had forgotten her.

But she looked up to find him standing over her with a tender look in his eyes. "Bye for now, sprout," he said. He reached into his jacket and pulled out a little box wrapped in brown paper. "This is for you," he told her, and pressed it into her hand. "Open it when you're alone."

He reached down and hugged her, and Cora threw her arms

around him and cried.

'We'll talk to you soon, sprout," he promised, and kissed her.

She watched them leave with a heavy heart: Joseph walked out the front door carrying Caleb in his arms, followed by their parents, and trailed by Emma and the boys. Hezekiah was munching a chicken leg, and Jeremy was play-boxing with his cousin, and was duly reprimanded by one of his uncles.

The throng of relatives blocked them from her sight, so Cora left the living room and climbed the stairs to her little corner bedroom, which overlooked the front porch. From her window, she could see them all climbing into the buggy, and Joes bundling Caleb up. Emma climbed into the front seat with Joes, and Hezekiah and Jeremy sat on either side of Caleb in the back -- Joes' idea, she was sure -- a human buffer to keep the rambunctious Caleb trapped in the back seat as he drove.

Joes leaned out and waved, and there was a loud chorus of farewells, and the buggy rolled out through the yard and took to the road. Cora watched it until it became a tiny speck on the horizon, and disappeared.

She flopped down on her bed, feeling low. Then she remembered the box that Joes had given her.

She pulled the wrapping paper back, to be astounded by

the sight of a brand-new cell phone. There was also a little card enclosed. She opened it and read:

Don't go crazy, sprout. Here's our number.

Cora gasped and fell back onto the bed. Then she hugged the phone to her chest, smiling from ear to ear.

CHAPTER EIGHTEEN

When it came time for Cora to return to work, she discovered that going back wasn't as simple as merely borrowing her sister's bicycle and pedaling into town.

On that first morning, she lingered in the bathroom for a full 10 minutes, staring at her dreadful hair, until one of her little nephews began shouting and beating on the door.

There was no help for it: she was just going to have to suck it up, and hope that nobody laughed right in her face -- though, she thought glumly, they were almost *sure* to laugh behind her back.

She was blue and silent all through breakfast, and was grateful that everybody else was too busy to notice. She didn't feel like coming up with an excuse for why she felt cranky.

She wasn't supposed to be worried about her *appearance*.

She skipped out of the house and across the yard, grabbing her sister's bicycle and launching off across the drive. *They might be wrong about other things,* Cora thought to herself grimly, *but that's something the English have right. Everybody cares about how they look, even if they don't admit it.*

It was a much longer trip to the schoolhouse now than it had been when she lived with Joes, and she got quite a workout by the time she rolled into the school yard.

She pulled to a stop, fighting the temptation to turn around and go back home. Her hair was chopped, wind-tangled, and ridiculous, and for a bonus – she was going to arrive *sweaty and winded,* as well.

Cora leaned the bicycle up against a tree, got her breath, and smoothed out her skirts. It took her a good five minutes to gather her nerve, but she finally did.

Well, I'm going to have to go in sooner or later, she told herself.

It was still early, and none of the children had arrived yet, but Cora could see the glow of lights in the windows: Fannie and Mary were already there.

She paused outside the doors, took a deep breath, and walked in.

To her relief, Fannie Stoltzfus was too polite to give any sign that she noticed anything out of the way in Cora's appearance. She smiled and came over and hugged her.

"Cora! I'm so glad you're feeling better," she smiled. "We've missed you, haven't we, Mary?" she cried, turning to her daughter.

Mary mumbled something too low to hear. Cora shrugged, thinking that, while Mary wasn't very polite, at least she wasn't acting any stranger this morning than she *usually* did.

***

Mrs. Stoltzfus sat Cora down, and asked about her hand, and made her tell how Caleb was doing. Cora noticed that Mrs. Stoltzfus was careful to avoid probing about Katie, and was silently grateful for her tact.

They talked for awhile, and finally settled down to the work of preparing the schoolroom for the day ahead: cleaning up, tidying papers and books, preparing materials.

The children began to trickle in, and Cora braced herself, thinking surely the sight of her chopped hair would provoke giggling and pointing. But to her surprise, the children paid no more heed to her scraggly hair than Fannie Stoltzfus.

By the time it was time to ring the bell for class, Cora was convinced that Mrs. Stoltzfus must have primed them beforehand with a lecture, and possibly threats.

So she was as shocked as anyone else, when, just before classes started, three little girls roiled the whole room by arriving at school with their hair chopped off under their ears -- *just like Cora.*

"Auch das noch!" Mary Stoltzfus cried.

Cora rolled her eyes, not knowing whether to be more amazed at the children's stunt, or that for *once* in her life, Mary Stoltzfus had been startled into *spontaneity.*

Fannie Stoltzfus recovered from her momentary speechlessness and pulled the little girls up to her desk.

"What have you done?" she wailed, turning their heads, "Why have you cut off all your beautiful hair?"

The three of them turned as one to look at Cora. They murmured, "Miss Cora is so brave and smart. We wanted to be *just like her* -- so we agreed to cut our hair!"

Mrs. Stoltzfus shook her head. "How, *how* did you do this without your mothers knowing?" she cried.

One little girl held up a pair of scissors with an expression of serene triumph. "We cut our hair out in the *schoolyard!"* Cora put her hands over her mouth and rolled her eyes to the little girls. They returned her gaze with frank hero worship.

Cora suddenly remembered what her little cousin had said, the comment she had ignored at the time: *Everyone in town thinks you're a hero.*

She could still hardly believe it was true -- but she couldn't deny the evidence of her own eyes.

Mrs. Stoltzfus took a deep breath. "Well, it can't be undone now. Children, go to your seats."

Then she came up to Cora, and said in a low voice: "You must tell the children not to do such things. You must tell them it isn't right to pay more attention to one person, than another."

To Cora's surprise, Mary chimed in, as well: "Yes, tell them that *you're no better than anyone else,* Cora Lapp!"

Fannie Stoltzfus turned and hissed an urgent rebuke into Mary's ears, but then turned back to Cora and nodded.

Cora's face was burning from Mary's rudeness, but for Fannie Stoltzfus' sake, and because it was the right thing to do, she stepped out reluctantly in front of the class and cleared her throat.

"Children, it's – it's not right to look up to me, as though one person could be more important than another. We are all the same. You should know that, by now."

Cora looked over at Fannie Stoltzfus, who nodded encouragement. Then she suddenly blurted: "I only cut my hair because it had been *burned.* I never thought that anyone would *copy* me!"

She looked over at the three little girls, and to her dismay, their expressions had not changed. They were still looking at her as if she had descended from the sky.

"So, um, that's all," she stammered, and quickly stepped back.

Mrs. Stoltzfus stepped up quickly and thanked Cora with a look of genuine gratitude. "Thank you, Cora," she said aloud. "And children, Cora is right. *We are all the same.*

"Now Mary, please bring me the lessons for the second grade scholars," she said briskly, and returned to her desk.

***

At noon, the recess bell rang, and it was Cora's turn to supervise the children as they played. She walked out into the schoolyard and sat down on the grass, watching as the children jumped and ran. To her dismay, her three little followers came and sat at her feet, and in spite of the lecture she read them, they wouldn't run off and play until Mary Stoltzfus arrived and told them sternly to go and talk to the other children.

Cora stared at her in surprise. It was rare for Mary to come out to recess when it wasn't her turn to supervise. But she didn't have long to wonder about it, because as soon as the children were gone, Mary rounded on her with fire in her eyes.

"You made a fine speech today, Cora Lapp," Mary said resentfully, "but you didn't mean a word of it, did you? You just said it because Mamm *made* you say it!"

Cora was taken aback by her vehemence. She had thought of Mary Stoltzfus as one of the most boring people she knew, a girl who didn't have the nerve to raise her eyes, much less her *voice*. She cocked her head at Mary and appraised her.

"I said it because it was the right thing to say, Mary Stoltzfus," she told her coolly. "And I don't care whether you believe it, or not."

"I *don't* believe it," Mary replied angrily. "You're a spoiled, selfish girl, Cora Lapp, and you're bad for these children. Why don't you just go home? Everyone would be better off, if you did!"

Then she jumped up and stormed back into the schoolroom.

Cora's face was tingling as if she'd been slapped. Such hateful treatment would ordinarily have driven her either to tears – or to a fight. But for the first time in Cora's life, *amazement* drove out all other emotions. She stared after her attacker in disbelief.

Who would've guessed it – that little mud hen, Mary Stoltzfus, had a *spine*!

She'd been very rude, of course, but Cora knew that it was bluster. Fannie Stoltzfus had offered her a permanent teaching position, and Cora suspected that Mary's hissy fit had more to do with *that*, than any great concern for the proprieties.

What was it that Isaac had said once – that Mary was

jealous of her? At the time, she hadn't given it much thought, but Isaac had good judgment, especially about people. It looked as if he'd been proved right.

Cora pulled a blade of grass out of the ground, turned it this way and that. In spite of Mary's rudeness, she suddenly felt sorry for her. For the last week, Cora had been self-conscious and unhappy because her short hair made her feel ugly. It had been humiliating, but it was only temporary. Her hair would grow back.

But Mary Stoltzfus was *plain*, every day and all day long, and not just because of her hair. She was skinny and grim and strange. She had never had a date, much less a boyfriend, and she was so odd that she didn't even have any friends.

Cora twirled the blade of grass. The sudden thought came to her: *It must be very hard to be Mary Stoltzfus.*

The sound of the children's voices snapped her out of her daydream. "Miss Cora, Miss Cora!" her little followers were crying, "Come and be on *our* team!"

CHAPTER NINETEEN

That night, Cora lay awake staring at her bedroom ceiling long after all the lights had gone out. She was still brooding about Mary Stoltzfus, and what she had said.

Cora tossed on her mattress. She was beginning to like her job, and she was confident that she was going to keep it. Fannie Stoltzfus was an honest person, and wouldn't withdraw an offer, once it was made.

Cora was beginning to like the children, too, and it looked as if they liked her. Fannie had told her that she was *happy* with her work at the school.

But that work still wasn't going to be very pleasant, or productive, if she and Mary couldn't get along.

Cora buried her face in her pillow. Oh, Lord, she prayed, Please be my friend. Tell me what to do. Is it my fault that this girl is jealous? I'm not after her job, and I haven't done anything to hurt her, but she still attacks me. Lord, I don't mean to be hateful, but seriously -- is she crazy?

Her poor mother!

She tossed over on her other side.

Lord, I've tried to be nice to Mary Stoltzfus, and she still acts like she wants to stab me. What else can I do?

There was no apparent answer, and Cora put her hands over her face, wishing that Isaac was there to hold her, to comfort her with his love and good sense. He had seen this coming, and had tried to warn her.

She saw him again in her mind, sitting next to her in the yard swing. She heard him saying: *"It might help, if you tried to get to know her outside of school."*

But the suggestion still depressed her. It was the sort of thing only *Isaac* would ever think of.

Oh, Isaac, she thought mournfully, you're a better person than I'll ever be!

And I wish you had a cell phone!

She turned over on her side again, sighed, and let that wistful thought gradually carry her off to sleep.

***

When she rose the next day, Cora got dressed and ready

for work with a grim sense of purpose. She had made up her mind what she was going to do. At this point, it was really her only choice.

She arrived at school, settled quietly into her routine, and performed her duties with admirable decorum, until the bell for recess.

Then she put her plan into action.

It was Mary's turn to go out and supervise the children at play, and as usual, she was sitting down on a bench watching them, without joining in or saying a word.

Cora finished her own tasks, but instead of making small talk with Fannie Stoltzfus, as she usually did at recess, she walked out to where Mary was sitting and plopped down on the bench beside her.

Mary sat in stony silence, ignoring her, until Cora said: "*I'm not going away, Mary.* We're going to have to work together. And it's silly for you and me to sit in class every day and stare each other down, like two cats."

Mary turned to face her. "Why are you even *here*? You don't want to be a teacher. You aren't trained to be a teacher. Why don't you just get married and forget about working? It's what you're best suited for!"

Cora bit her lip and looked away. "*I'll* be the judge of what I want to do, and what I'm suited for. And I'm telling you plainly that I *like* teaching here, and that you may as well make the best of me."

She turned and stared Mary straight in the eye.

"*Oh!*" Mary cried in exasperation, and flounced back to the classroom.

And for the rest of the day, Mary ignored her, didn't speak to her, and didn't give any indication that she even knew that Cora was there.

But Cora had determined that Mary's stubbornness wasn't going to get the best of *her*.

Every day that week, she made a point of making small talk with Mary in class, or following her out to recess. Her only reward for her trouble had been repeated tongue lashings, and a lot of accusations.

After the fourth day of this strategy, Mary had snapped: "Are you trying to *take over*, Cora Lapp? I know what you're after – you think that *you'll* be the teacher here one day, and that you can push me out. Well, I won't let you. You've gotten your own way with everything *else*, but you're not getting *this!*"

Cora forced herself to sit quietly, though she had begun to fantasize about slapping Mary Stoltzfus right to the moon. She snapped: "I think *no such thing*, Mary Stoltzfus. You're crazier than a bag of bats!"

The result had been more insults, Mary flouncing back

inside, and Mary pretending that Cora didn't exist, for the rest of the day.

But Cora noticed that Fannie Stoltzfus, at least, was watching. She said nothing, but Cora could feel her quiet gaze even when she was turned away.

She got the sense that Fannie knew what was going on – and that she was paying *very* close attention.

***

By the end of the week, Cora had to admit that five days of confrontation had resulted in a lot of painful honesty, but no improvement. It still amazed her, but wimpy little Mary Stoltzfus was proving to be a lot tougher than she looked.

But Cora was determined not to give up.

It was time for *Phase Two*.

On Saturday morning, Cora rose early and helped her mother cook breakfast. In addition to all the biscuits and pancakes and muffins they made, Cora baked a big, beautiful loaf of Friendship Bread, and beat all the children back from it with a wooden spoon.

"Get your hands away! I'm taking it to a –"

She hesitated, because she had to stop and consider what Mary should be *called*.

"To Fannie Stoltzfus," she finished quickly.

When the bread was hot and fragrant and filled the house with the aroma of cinnamon, Cora wrapped it up in a cloth and put it in a cardboard box.

Then she kissed her mother and ran out the door, telling her that she was going visiting.

The Stoltzfus farm wasn't all that far away from the Lapp's, a fairly easy ride on a bicycle. Cora reached the farm in less than 20 minutes, and was gratified to see that the buggy was still sitting in the yard. She had no fear that Mary might be off somewhere on her own: Mary never went *anywhere* unless she was dragged there by others.

She knocked on the front door, and after a few minutes Fannie Stoltzfus came to answer it, wiping her hands on a dish cloth. She looked surprised to see Cora, and genuinely pleased.

"Why Cora, how nice to see you!" she exclaimed, and held the door open. "Come in! I was just thinking how nice it would be to see you sometime after work, and here you are!"

Cora held out the load of bread. It still smelled wonderfully of cinnamon and sugar.

"I brought this for Mary," Cora told her. "Is she here?"

For an instant, Fannie Stoltzfus stared at her in frank astonishment, before recovering her poise. "Well, that's very sweet of you, Cora," she replied softly. "You can take it to her yourself. She's in the dining room. She's working on a quilt. Maybe you'd like to help her?"

"I'd be glad to," Cora replied.

Fannie Stoltzfus took the bread from Cora's hands, promising to return with coffee and plates. Cora ventured through the living room to the Stoltzfus dining room, and sure enough, there was Mary, pulling a needle through a quilt square.

Cora cleared her throat, and Mary looked up and jumped almost comically.

"*What are you* –" she began, but cut herself off because her mother entered suddenly with cake and coffee.

"Mary, Cora came over and brought you some friendship bread," Fannie cooed, smiling over her shoulder at Cora. "Wasn't that thoughtful? I asked her to help you with your quilting, and she said she would."

Mary looked down at her hands and murmured, "Thank you, Cora," in a flat tone.

Fannie beamed at them. "Well, I have things to do, so I'll leave you two to your quilting. But call me if you'd like anything, Cora."

Cora smiled after her, and when she was gone, turned her eyes to Mary.

Mary jerked a needle savagely through a quilt square. "*Why are you here?*" she hissed. "Why are you pretending that we're *friends*? You're just trying to suck up to my mother!"

Cora eyed her grimly. "I'm here because I'm hoping we might *become* friends, Mary," she said evenly.

"You're not my friend," Mary growled, "you just want things to be easier for you at work."

Cora paused, and had to admit that Mary had her *there*, but rallied:

"I'm *trying* to be friendly, I really am, but you aren't making things very easy for me. I came all the way over here, on a *Saturday*, to bring you a present -- and you bite my head off!

"Don't you *want* any friends?" she blurted in frustration.

To Cora's surprise, Mary's angry bravado cracked momentarily. She looked down quickly, but not before Cora caught a glint in her eye.

Cora heard Isaac's patient words again in her memory, and said, more kindly:

"I'll make you a deal, Mary Stoltzfus. I will *swear*, with my hand on the *Bible*, that I will never try to push you out of your job at the school, if you will swear that you'll try to act like a *human being*, instead of a jealous cat!"

She narrowed her eyes, and extended one hand, slowly and warily.

Mary looked at her out of the corner of her eye, pinched her lips together, and hesitated for a long moment.

"Well, *decide!*" Cora snapped.

Mary shrugged suddenly, grabbed two of her fingers, shook them limply, and let go.

Cora sat back in her chair, stifling a gasp.

Her English friends called this sort of thing a *Hail Mary*, because it usually didn't work.

But Cora decided not to question providence. She nodded, as if she had *expected* agreement, picked up a quilting needle, and began to sew.

321- 1470

thur Sept 8

8:30

CHAPTER TWENTY

When she finally came back from the Stoltzfus farm, Cora pulled the bicycle over to the side of the road and buried herself among the new corn stalks at the edge of her father's fields. Once she was safely among them, no one could see or hear her from the house.

She pulled out the cell phone and punched in Joes' number. To her relief, he picked up almost right away.

"Joes?" she cried.

"Hello, sprout," he said, and he sounded almost like his old self. Cora drank in the sound of her big brother's voice. After the morning she'd had, it was like a soothing tonic.

"Oh, Joes, thank you so much for this phone. I love it! I've been meaning to call you and ask about Katie, but there's been drama at the school and I got distracted. Don't ask – I'll tell you later.

"How's everyone doing? Did Katie go to the doctor? Is Caleb doing all right?"

"Katie's much better, and so is Caleb," he told her.

"How did Katie's visit go?"

"I took Katie to the counselor last week, and I think he really helped her," he answered slowly. "We both learned things. I never knew before just how brave Katie is. She's been keeping a lot of pain inside, for a long time."

His voice softened, and he fell silent, before finally adding: "But now she can let go of it. It helps her to talk. She's supposed to go back in a few weeks for another visit."

"How – how about the baby, Joes?" Cora asked softly.

"The doctor says the baby is fine," he assured her. "Katie's eating again now, and she's resting. In fact, she doesn't like how *much* we make her rest, but it's doctor's orders at the Lapp house these days."

"Oh, Joes, I'm so glad. It sounds like she's almost back on her feet."

"She's getting there," she agreed.

Cora lowered her voice, even though there wasn't a soul in sight. "Joes, did you – did you give Isaac my note?"

"Yes, I gave him your note," Joes sighed. "He came over the other day and was asking for you."

"I haven't heard from him for a *long time*," she replied. "I was beginning to wonder if there was something *wrong!*"

"You haven't heard from him in a *week*," Joseph corrected. "And he's been busy. I don't know what he's doing, but I've seen him around a lot. He drove past with a couple of strangers last week, and yesterday I saw him in town with that Hauser girl, what's her name –"

Cora stood up straight. "*Leah Hauser?*" she asked sharply.

"Yes, that's the one," Joes replied. "Don't flare up, sprout."

Cora shrugged. "Oh, I'm not worried," she assured him. "Leah Hauser likes to make a fool of herself in public, that's all, and Isaac's too polite to tell her to go away."

"I'm sure that's it."

Cora chewed her nail, and took so long to say anything that Joes' voice had to remind her that he was still on the phone.

"Joes, are you and Katie going to be at meeting this Sunday?" she asked suddenly.

"Yes, I think she's well enough to start back," he told her. "She misses you."

"Can I talk to her?" Cora asked.

"No," he replied.

"Why not?" Cora objected, and was startled to hear him

laugh.

"Because she doesn't know that we have a phone."

Cora dimpled, but was quick to add: "That's all right, Joes -- but if you see Isaac again, give the phone to him and *ask him to call me*."

"It's supposed to be for *emergencies*," he told her briskly. "And no, I don't think that a separation of seven days qualifies!"

"Oh, Joes, that's cold. I'm going to call you back when you're in a better mood," she giggled, and hung up.

***

But as she made her way back toward the house, Cora stayed inside the corn field to avoid being seen. She wanted some time alone to mull over what Joes had told her.

Leah Hauser with Isaac, yet *again*. And here she was, stuck on the other side of the county! The mental image of Leah Hauser clinging to Isaac's arm made her almost sick.

She wondered what Isaac had been busy doing, but she was just going to have to wait until he told her himself, tomorrow night at the sing.

Cora sighed. It would be the first Sunday meeting since she'd cut off all her hair, and she dreaded the stares and comments she would surely get. She closed her eyes and wished for the thousandth time that she was allowed at least a curling iron and a bag of makeup. Then she could at least try to *soften* the unflattering effect.

Isaac was so sweet and caring, he never made her feel like anything less than a princess, but as she walked the bicycle through the corn rows, Cora mourned the loss of her English freedoms.

She was going to look *terrible* tomorrow, and Leah Hauser would be quick to take advantage. Cora shook her head, fretting about it.

She wanted to *knock Isaac's socks off*, and with her ugly hair, she was *so* not going to.

As she prepared for her meeting with him, Cora would have given $500 for some glossy blonde hair extensions -- and a little black dress that didn't flare out from the waist.

The next morning, bright and early, Cora and her parents and her brothers and sisters and in laws and nieces and nephews all piled into buggies and took to the road for meeting. There were more than ten buggies in all, and soon they were joined by others on the road, all heading to the Miller's farm.

It was going to be a mild, beautiful day, and in spite of her sorry appearance, Cora was looking forward to the meeting. She couldn't wait to see Katie and Joes, and to cuddle Caleb, and to see Emma and the boys.

And she wondered how she was going to be able to see Isaac without throwing herself into his arms, right in front of *everybody*.

***

The Miller's farm was huge, bigger even than her parent's, and for once, there was room for everybody. A good thing, too, because it looked to Cora as if everybody had shown up. The Miller yard, and the road outside, was jammed with buggies.

Meeting had been set up in the massive barn, with rows on rows of folding chairs, but no one was sitting yet. They all stood around, talking and laughing.

Cora scanned the crowd for Isaac, but there was no sign of the Mullers yet. But then she caught sight of Joes' hat bobbing above the crowd. At six feet plus, it was hard to miss him.

Cora went running through the crowd, only to find that it was impossible to get to Joes: he was holding Caleb in his arms, and was surrounded by caps and bonnets. It looked to Cora as if all of the grandmothers within 20 yards were playing with Caleb's feet, straightening his sleeves, or threatening to kiss him.

"Katie!"

Katie turned around, and her face lit up at the sight of

Cora. She opened her arms, and Cora flew into them.

"You look *wonderful!*" Cora sighed in relief. And she did: Katie's pretty face was still a little pale, but a faint color had returned to her cheeks, and she was smiling.

"Oh, I've missed you!" Katie exclaimed.

Then Emma stepped up and hugged her, and even the boys came close, though they offered nothing like a *hug*: they looked at her, and then looked down at the ground, and kicked it with their feet.

"I'm so glad you came today," Katie told her, taking her hand. "You'll have to tell Isaac Muller that he's out of luck, because you're going to sit with *us*."

Cora laughed, but that reminded her: where *was* Isaac? She scanned the crowd for him, but there were so many people it was impossible to find him.

"You're going to have to stop looking, Cora," Katie told her wryly. "It's time to start."

So Cora followed Katie and Joes and sat down with them as meeting started. She kept turning her head, looking this way and that, but couldn't see him. Finally, an elderly woman behind Cora caught her eye and gave her such a quelling look that Cora had to turn around, and stay turned.

***

As the singing began, Cora closed her eyes, feeling vibrantly, unexpectedly *happy*: Katie and Caleb were going to be *all right*, and Joes was his old self again. She had found a job here, one that she really loved, and it looked like Mary Stoltzfus might – possibly -- *not* attack her on Monday.

And to Cora's surprise, when the deacon got up and began to talk, and she knew he was going to be there for *two hours*, this time, even *that* didn't bother her.

She began to *listen* to what he said, and for the first time, it made *sense*.

For the first time in her life, Cora felt that God wasn't mad at her. That He was actually a *friend*.

She could pledge her heart to a *friend*.

She hugged herself, smiling. She could picture it, now: she could see Cora Lapp joining the church, and settling down, and marrying Isaac Muller, and teaching at the school.

She could see herself being happy here, even if that meant she had to wear the dowdy clothes. If Isaac could kiss her and tell her that he loved her when her hair was chopped off and smelly of smoke, then she need not fear a plain dress.

At least, Cora told herself, I can still wear sexy underwear.

***

When the meeting was finally over, Cora couldn't wait to

find Isaac. *At last* she could tell him what she'd wanted to, all along. She smiled, imagining the joy on his face, and set out to find him.

Cora pushed through the crowd, craning her head this way and that, but none of the black hats had Isaac's face under them. She worked the whole perimeter, without luck, and down the center, and finally sat down on the front steps of the Miller farmhouse, stumped.

Mary Stoltzfus happened to be sitting on one of the porch chairs – alone, as usual. Cora gave her a quizzical look, and Mary jerked a thumb in the direction of the garden.

Cora nodded, and brushed out her skirt, and went to the garden.

At first she didn't see anyone, but the sound of low voices drew her to the little gazebo on the far end. There were two people standing in it: Isaac, at last! – and -- *Leah Hauser*.

All the joy drained out of Cora.

Leah leaned toward Isaac and put her hand on his arm, and the sight was just as revolting as Cora had imagined. Isaac laughed – a *real* laugh, she was quick to note -- not just a polite one.

Then, to her horror, Leah Hauser leaned forward and *kissed Isaac on the cheek.*

Cora watched in outrage, waiting for Isaac to pull back, to

protest, to walk away. But he just *stood there*, looking down at his shoes.

Cora felt a strangled scream rising up in her throat. She didn't wait to see more, because if she did, she was going to rush the gazebo like a mad thing and *choke Leah Hauser unconscious*.

She turned on her heel and stalked off. As she passed by the porch, she saw Mary Stoltzfus' black bonnet lying on the floor. Without a word, she snatched it up and crammed it down over her head, because she was going home if she had to walk, and she didn't want anyone else to see that she was crying.

CHAPTER TWENTY-ONE

Halfway down the Miller's long driveway, Cora met Hezekiah and Jeremy as they kicked a soccer ball back and forth.

They stopped doing it to look at her, and she snapped: "Well, which one of you is going to drive me home?" She didn't even try to disguise the fact that she had been crying: it was pointless.

They looked at her, and at one another, and Hezekiah held out his hand.

"Come on, then," he said.

The two boys walked her out to Joes' buggy, and they had barely gotten in, when Hezekiah suddenly dropped the reins. He had twisted around, was looking at something behind them.

"Please go on!" Cora begged him, but instead, both of the

boys abandoned the buggy without a word and *left her sitting there*.

"Oh!" Cora shrieked, feeling that she had endured her limit. She was just about to get up and take the reins herself, when *at last*, she came face to face with Isaac.

He climbed into the front seat and sat there for a minute before saying anything, and Cora was in no mood to help him.

Finally, he murmured: "Mary Stoltzfus told me that you stole her bonnet."

"Did she tell you *why*?" Cora snapped.

"Cora, I don't know what you saw –" he began, but she cut him off.

"I saw *more than enough*, Isaac Muller," she cried. "I saw Leah Hauser *lay hands on you*, and then *kiss* you! And I saw you *standing there laughing*, as if it happened every day!"

"It wasn't what it looked like," he told her quietly. "You don't understand."

"What *is* there to understand, Isaac?" she asked him tearfully. "After *the note I sent you*, you didn't show me your face to me for a week! I had to come *here* to find you, and when I *did* find you, you were hiding in a gazebo, *kissing Leah Hauser*!"

"I *never* kissed her," he broke in, but Cora waved him off.

"Oh, go away, Isaac," she sobbed, "I can't stand to look at your face – it's got Leah Hauser's fingerprints all over it!"

"Cora, you know as well as I do that Leah Hauser is – *forward*," Isaac said carefully. "What did you want me to do, push her out of the gazebo?"

"*Yes!*" Cora cried.

"We've been together since we were children," Isaac pleaded. "You know me as well as anyone. Have I *ever* shown any interest in Leah Hauser?"

"Joes told me that you were in town with her just this *week*!" she retorted.

He looked down at his hands. "No, Joseph saw her *attach* herself to me," he said softly, "just like *you* did."

"And neither one of us saw you *struggle*!" Cora cried.

Isaac fell silent, and then resumed, evenly: "Cora, when I got your note, I knew that I had things to do, things I had to finish, before I could see you again. The reason you haven't heard anything from me, all week, is that I was busy in town. I was searching for a *house*."

Cora stopped sobbing – very amazement had conquered her tears.

"Cora, I rented a house in town. A house for *you and me*."

He reached over the seat and took her hand. "Cora, this

time, let me *finish* asking. You know I love you, and you love me. I want us to be *married*, Cora. Is that answer enough for you? I want us to take our kneeling vows this summer and be *married*."

His big, blue eyes were on hers, pleading with her, and it took all of Cora's will power to resist the look in them.

But she summoned up her very last ounce. *Some things were beyond even a pair of beautiful blue eyes.*

She snatched her hand out of his. "Well, all I can say, Isaac Muller," she began incredulously, "is that you have a funny way of asking me to marry you – on the same day – no, *the same hour* – that I catch you with another girl!"

Isaac clenched his jaw, a sure sign that he was feeling tested, but by this time, Cora was past caring.

"I wouldn't marry you, if you were the richest man in the county," she went on, swiping at his cheek with her fingertips, "because Leah Hauser's tacky lipstick is *still on your face*, and a fine Amish wife she would make too, ignoring the *ordnung* that way, and probably flirting with other men behind your back, and it would *serve you right* if she did, because then you'd know *exactly* how I feel today!"

Isaac's lips tightened to a straight line. "Cora, *I know you're upset*, but I've already told you how it was. After all we've been through together, I'd have thought I would've earned more of your *trust*."

Cora calmed down a bit, because it *was* a just objection. In spite of what she'd just seen, Cora knew very well that Isaac was a good man. She weakened. She looked up at him through swimming eyes, and turned her lower lip down.

He took her hand again, and leaned in to kiss her, and she was turning her face up a *tiny* bit to meet his, when the sound of Leah Hauser's voice calling made them both freeze.

"*Isaac, where are you?*" she was calling.

"Well, what are you staring at *me* for?" Cora asked coldly, and pushed him away. "*There's* your girlfriend calling, Isaac Muller! Don't keep her waiting!"

Isaac looked at her with genuine frustration in his eyes. It was the first time in her life Cora had ever seen him look *mad*.

"Well, at least there are *some* girls in the world who *know what they want*, Cora Lapp," he told her angrily. "This is the *fourth time* I've tried to ask you to marry me, and the *fourth time* you've sent me away!

"Maybe I might have better luck, *if I asked someone else!*"

"*Oh!*" Cora screamed, but she was balked of a crushing reply, because Isaac stalked off. Cora twisted around to watch him go, and to her chagrin, Leah Hauser met him and grabbed his arm again. As they walked off, Isaac looked back over his shoulder, and then *put his arm around her*.

Cora squeezed her eyes and her fists together and beat the back of poor Joseph's buggy to a pulp, but it didn't help at all.

There was no way to un-see Isaac, *with his arm around another girl.*

CHAPTER TWENTY-TWO

The next day at recess, Cora sat glumly on the playground bench. Her fury with Isaac had melted quickly into the blues.

On *this* day, she had no intention of seeking out Mary Stoltzfus for light conversation. But to her surprise, Mary came to *her*.

"Have you got my bonnet?" she asked.

Cora nodded wordlessly, and slapped it into Mary's outstretched hand. But to Cora's dull surprise, Mary didn't go away. She sat down on the bench beside her and looked up at the clouds.

"You know, I wouldn't worry about it," Mary said at last. "They walked right past me, and the look on his face reminded me of a second grader, when I talk about math. I don't think he heard a word she said."

Cora looked at her, cracked the ghost of a smile, and shook

her head. "Thank you."

Maybe it was the lack of judgment, for once, or the sympathetic tone in Mary's voice. But to her own surprise, Cora suddenly heard herself pouring out her troubles to *Mary Stoltzfus*.

"Maybe it wasn't meant to be," she murmured sadly. "We just can't seem to get together. I've had a real hard time trying to fit in here. I don't know if I can do it, or even if I want to -- you know?"

Mary nodded, and the thought occurred to Cora that maybe she *did* know.

"And then, too, I spent some time out among the English, and in some ways they're so *free*. I loved being able to dress nice and wear makeup and travel around and see new places. I still miss that sometimes, you know?"

Mary shot Cora an odd, appraising look, and then answered: "Yes. I mean, I can imagine. I – I've always wanted to travel, myself. I've always wanted to see New York."

Cora looked at her and shrugged. "So why don't you do it? It's your rumspringa, isn't it?"

Mary shook her head. "I can't. *I can't*. I get terrified every time I think of it!"

"Why?"

Mary looked at her as if she'd lost her mind. *"Why?* Because I'm afraid that something might happen to me, like happened to you, Cora Lapp!" She shook her head. "The world is so *dangerous,*" she murmured.

Cora shook her head. "Well, I have news for you, Mary," she sighed. "You can't hide from trouble by staying *here,* that's for sure. And you can't really make up your mind whether you want to be Amish or English, until you've lived both ways, and had a chance to compare."

Mary squinted her eyes almost as if she was in pain. "I wish I had your nerve, Cora Lapp," she sighed. "I'd go to New York, or even –" she broke off hopelessly.

"Well, what hinders you?" Cora asked. "You've got some money saved, don't you?"

"Yes, but I can hardly go *alone,*" Mary retorted, "and there's no one –" She bit her lip and looked down.

Cora sighed, appraised her sympathetically. *Mary Stoltzfus wanted to go to New York.*

Needed to go to New York, more probably, because it seemed to Cora that Mary needed some kind of therapy -- almost like Katie's.

Mary needed to learn how *not to be afraid.*

And she had no one to help her learn.

Cora looked down at her hands. *She* was available, if they

could keep it to a day trip. She had her own little stash of money, enough for tickets. And her only alternative – sitting miserably at home for the weekend, wondering if Leah Hauser was pawing Isaac – made a trip with Mary Stoltzfus seem almost a *pleasure* by comparison.

She looked over at Mary and shrugged.

"*I* could go with you," she said.

Mary looked at her, and looked again, and cracked a tiny smile. "Will you have a problem getting your parents to agree?" she asked.

Cora shook her head. "No. You?"

"Probably not."

Cora nodded. "Meet me at my house early next Saturday morning with money, and sunglasses, and a backpack. Wear comfortable shoes."

Mary narrowed her eyes. "You *better not* be playing me, Cora Lapp," she warned.

"*Just be there*," Cora told her.

***

When Cora proposed the idea of a day trip to New York, her daed refused out of hand.

At first.

And then she went and sat on the arm of his chair, and wheedled, and begged, and promised, and he still said *no*.

Unless there was someone with her that they knew.

And then she told him Mary Stoltzfus was going too, and he said it was like having no one else at all, because she couldn't take care of herself, much less anyone else.

And Cora was shocked that he thought so little of the *town schoolteacher*, who had read *so many books*, and was such a *conscientious member of the community*.

And then he had to take *back* some of the things he'd said, but still didn't like the idea, until she pointed out that it would be an *educational* trip.

To Cora's delight, her mother came unexpectedly to her aid.

"Oh, let her go, Amon," she soothed. "It's rumspringa. They're almost *grown* now."

He had looked at her with a grim glint in his eye, but finally caved. "I can't argue with the both of you," he sighed, and threw up his hands. "God help me."

His wife kissed him, but he shook his head.

"She always gets her way with me," he told her. "Sometimes I think *you* taught her how to do it!"

"I could, Amon," his wife agreed, smiling. "I've been

honing my technique for thirty years."

CHAPTER TWENTY-THREE

By 10 o'clock on Saturday morning, Cora and Mary were sitting side by side on a bus bound for New York. To Cora, that old, familiar sense of adventure was like a friend she hadn't seen in a long time. She leaned back into her seat, savoring it. It felt *good* to be travelling again.

After awhile she looked over at Mary. When they had first boarded the bus, she had frankly been afraid that Mary was going to get sick. She had looked weird and scared and she hadn't said a word since they sat down.

But now she looked like she was beginning to relax.

"I brought some English clothes in my backpack," Cora told her. "We should change at the terminal."

"What kind of clothes?" Mary asked tremulously.

"Jeans, tees. You can borrow a pair. I also brought some makeup. I can do your face, if you like."

Mary raised her eyebrows, looking scandalized. Then she cracked a crooked little smile.

"*Heh heh heh heh heh!*" she cackled, and Cora had to bite her lip.

***

When they arrived at the New York terminal, Mary began to look scared again, and Cora had to admit that *she* wasn't feeling all that brave, either. The din was deafening, and she had never seen so many people in her life. The terminal looked and smelled dirty, but the bathroom was the only place they had to change, so they went in.

Cora tossed a pair of jeans and a tee shirt to Mary, and dressed quickly in one of her own favorite English outfits. The feel of jeans was like – well, like letting her hair down. Cora sank down onto a bench and sighed.

She looked up at Mary. Her clothes were a bit too big for Mary, but it was odd: Mary looked *better* in them. Cora fished in her bag and made Mary stand in front of the mirror.

"Here, let me fix your hair," she commanded, and Mary let her pick the pins out of it. Cora pulled it loose, and brushed it, and considered Mary Stoltzfus in the mirror.

"You know, you're not –" she bit her lip.

"You can say it," Mary replied, in an ironic tone. "Not *that* bad?"

"I'm going to try something," Cora told her, and began working with the brush. She pulled Mary's hair back into a waterfall, and brushed little tendrils down behind each ear.

"You know, that looks *much* nicer, Mary," she told her.

Then she fished in the bag again, and pulled out a makeup brush and some mascara.

"Stand still," she told her.

She worked on Mary's face for about five minutes. After Cora had finished drawing and painting, to their mutual amazement, Mary Stoltzfus looked – if not *beautiful* – at least, something not so far from *pretty*.

Cora looked at Mary's face and smiled. Her companion's expression said *I can't believe it* better than any words.

"Where do you want to go first?" Cora asked.

***

They strolled down the sidewalks of Times Square, with Mary reading off a travel brochure. "I want to see the Empire State building," she was saying, "and the Metropolitan Museum, *at least*."

"And we have to stop somewhere for lunch," Cora added.

"Then I want to see the Guggenheim and the Statue of Liberty," Mary added.

"We only have a few hours," Cora reminded her.

"And Central Park and the zoo," she finished, and crushed the paper to her chest. "Oh, Cora, I can't believe I'm *really* here!"

Cora smiled at her. Mary was getting over her shyness fast, and already looked like a different person from the awkward, skinny little girl back home.

"So let's go have fun," she told her, and they hailed a cab.

***

They went to the Metropolitan Museum first, and while Cora didn't get much out of paintings and statues, she got a big kick out of watching *Mary* watch them. Mary Stoltzfus wandered from room to room in the museum, looking as if she was afraid she might wake up and find it had all been a dream. Occasionally she cried out and grabbed Cora's arm.

"Oh Cora! It's the famous Van Gogh!"

Or: "*Look!* It's a genuine *Da Vinci!*"

Then she dragged Cora to the gift shop, and spent what Cora thought was an exorbitant amount of money on a glossy magazine filled with photos of the artwork.

"I want to remember this for as long as I *live*," she told Cora breathlessly.

Then they went to Central Park, and visited the zoo. Cora

had never been to one before, and was delighted by the exotic animals. Once a tiny, fuzzy monkey seemed to notice her, and jumped right up to the edge of the enclosure to scream and clap its hands. Both of them burst out laughing.

As they walked out of the zoo, Cora checked her watch. "If you want to see the Empire State building, we'd better go soon," she warned. "It's almost four now, and it takes awhile to get in. Plus, I'm starving! We need to get something to *eat*!"

There was a hot dog stand nearby, and they stopped for a quick bite on the way. They ate on the sidewalk while they waited for a cab, and Cora fumbled with her wallet.

To her horror, suddenly Cora felt a sharp, cold pressure in her lower back. A low, rough voice behind her hissed: "*Give me that wallet. Now!*"

But Cora didn't have a chance to reply, because there was a quick scuffle, and she turned just in time to see Mary Stoltzfus shove the mugger right out into oncoming traffic. He fell down, rolled, and had to scramble up and run across the street as tires squealed and horns blared.

Cora turned in amazement to look at Mary, and Mary looked as if she'd shocked herself.

"*Thank you*, Mary," Cora gasped, and then shook her head. "You've been holding *out* on us!" she blurted.

***

The two of them took a minute or two to regain their nerve, and then caught a cab to the Empire State. They had to stand in line, but after a half hour they were on their way up. Cora didn't especially like heights, and the elevator ride made her feel a bit strange, but when they got to the top, and stepped out onto the observation deck, she had to admit that the *whole trip* had been worth it.

The vast, byzantine city stretched out before her, down to the glittering Hudson River, and beyond, all the way to the horizon. They could see the very curve of the earth.

"There's the Statue of Liberty!" Mary cried, pointing.

Cora stood with her fingers curled around the railings, thinking sadly, *Oh, Isaac, I wish you were here. I wish you could see this.*

But I'd rather see the inside of your house, than all the towers and museums in the world.

CHAPTER TWENTY-FOUR

They arrived back at home very late, far after midnight. But before they parted, Mary astounded Cora by reaching out and giving her a hug.

"You know, I was wrong about you, Cora Lapp," she said softly. "You're a decent person, and you've given me a day I'll never forget. *Thank you.*"

"I think I was wrong about you, too, Mary," Cora told her, and smiled. "I'll see you on Monday –*killer*!"

When she got home, she dragged into the dark house and sneaked upstairs, trying not to make any noise.

Then she flopped down on her bed and was asleep almost as soon as she fell.

***

The next day was Sunday. But when Cora woke up, she saw that the rest of the family had mercifully allowed her to oversleep, and had gone to church without her.

She groaned and stretched and rolled over, smiling. *Who would've thought it*, she yawned, still thinking of Mary Stoltzfus, and the mugger who'd found out the hard way that she was tougher than she looked.

Wait until she told Isaac!

But then she opened her eyes, remembering that *she and Isaac weren't on speaking terms.*

Cora picked at her bed sheet. Their fight had been stupid, and she already regretted it. But she wasn't going to go crawling on her knees to Isaac and beg him to take her back.

No, *he* was going to be the one to make the first move.

She threw off her bedcovers and knelt down on the floor, pulling a dusty suitcase out from under it.

If scrawny little Mary Stoltzfus could beat off a mugger on the mean streets of New York, then, Cora told herself, *she could fight for her man.*

Get ready, Leah, she thought grimly, and headed for the bathroom.

***

That evening, Cora walked softly down the back stairs of her parent's house and slipped out onto the road. There was a youth sing that evening, and luckily not very far away.

Close enough to walk.

Cora's hair ruffled softly in the evening breeze. She'd spent hours combing and curling and spraying it, and now she could honestly say that it looked as good as it ever had in her life.

She'd made up her face like one of those paintings she'd seen in the museums, the ones where the woman's cheeks glowed like the pink lip of a seashell. She'd feathered her lashes lightly and thoroughly, and now they were as thick and soft as Caleb's.

And she had finally found a little black dress she *liked*.

***

When she arrived at the sing, Cora entered quietly and sat down on a bench without a word to anyone.

Mary Stoltzfus was there, and Cora had to repress a smile, because she was wearing English clothes. Mary was in a pair of jeans and a tee shirt, and was wearing the same hairstyle and makeup that Cora had given her.

To Cora's relief, Isaac was there, too. He was sitting on a bench across the room, looking patently miserable. Cora shifted her weight slightly and crossed one long leg over another.

She glanced at Isaac through her lashes, and was gratified to see that he'd noticed her. He was staring at her with so much intensity in his eyes that she felt almost alarmed. Was it anger, *still*?

But she had come to be *seen* by Isaac, not to *talk* to him.

Cora turned her eyes on the real object of her mission – *Leah Hauser*.

Leah was sitting on a bench a few rows down from Cora, and her smug expression had quickly curdled when she saw Cora glide in, wearing a black bombshell number right off the pages of a fashion magazine, and with hair as perfect as a model's.

Leah crossed her legs and arms, looking angrily to one side of the room.

Cora watched Leah's reaction with grim satisfaction. She was also aware that every male in the room had his eyes glued to her face, but she kept her own turned demurely down, as if she was reading her hymnal.

All during the sing, she made eye contact with no one. She stole an occasional glance at Isaac, but even then, only through her lashes. He was looking down at his hymnal, and not even pretending to sing.

When the singing was over, Cora uncrossed her legs, and went straight to Leah Hauser's side.

"I'd like a word with you *outside*," she told her quietly.

Leah looked up at her in surprise. "I don't have anything to say to you, Cora Lapp," she shrugged.

But Cora leaned in and whispered: *"It's about Isaac Muller."*

Leah glanced up at her, tossed her head, and reluctantly rose. Cora led her out through a side door, and out across the yard to a little barn on the far side of it.

"Where are you going?" Leah called impatiently. "And why do you think I want to hear you talk?"

But Cora merely opened the barn door, and beckoned for Leah to follow.

***

When Leah entered the barn, she crossed her arms and demanded: "What's this all about? Have you come to ask me to stop seeing Isaac Muller? Because it you have, it won't work."

Cora's eyes narrowed. "No, I haven't come to ask you anything," she said sweetly, "I've come to beat your two eyes into *one!*"

She kicked off her flimsy heels, and pulled her hair back from her face.

Leah stared at her with an expression of amused disbelief. "What are you going to do, beat Isaac up, *too?*"

"That won't be necessary," Cora told her. She braced her

bare feet on the wooden floor, and crooked a finger at her rival. "Throw *down*, Leah!"

Leah's eyes widened. "You're crazy!" she exclaimed, "Do you think Isaac wants a woman who goes around beating other people up? Isaac wants an Amish wife – and you'll *never* be Amish, Cora Lapp!"

"I'm not Amish *yet*," Cora corrected her. She smiled at Leah grimly. "I'm still on my *rumspringa*. I'll repent all day tomorrow, but I'm going to kick your can *tonight*!"

Leah shrieked and turned to run, but Cora caught her by the heel and tripped her, and they both fell heavily on the floor. Cora grabbed a handful of Leah's hair and yanked it out, and Leah shrieked with rage and slapped her across the jaw.

For answer, Cora yanked Leah to her feet and hurled her across the room.

"Isaac Muller has asked me to marry him *four* times," Cora panted, "he's rented a house and asked me to come *live* in it, and he will *be my husband* before Christmas. And I'm warning you, Leah Hauser – if I see you so much as *look* in his direction, *ever again*, I'll make you wish you'd never been born!"

Leah screamed, picked up a can of paint lying on a shelf, and hurled it at Cora. It narrowly missed her head and broke a row of mason jars.

Cora rolled up her sleeves, and flung herself at Leah again. Her palm made solid contact with Leah's jaw at least five times before her rival screamed, threw her hands up in the air, and fled the barn, wailing.

Cora chased her to the barn door, panting -- but she had driven the enemy from the field.

And when she turned to go back into the barn, she was startled to see Mary Stoltzfus standing quietly at the entrance, for all the world like a – *guard*.

She glanced at Cora, waved her fingers faintly, and walked off without saying a word.

***

Cora watched her go, and then turned back into the barn to get her shoes. But when she bent over to pick them up, she noticed a tall shadow in the corner.

"How long have you been standing there?" she asked.

"Long enough, Cora Lapp," Isaac answered.

"Why didn't you *say* something?" she demanded, putting her hands on her hips.

"I was afraid you'd beat *me, too*," he deadpanned, then added: "*So* – You say you're going to come and live in my house? And we're going to be married *before Christmas*?"

Cora flushed, and crossed her arms, and looked away.

But Isaac came over and took her into his arms. "Well, I may have to think about it for awhile, before I can answer." He put a hand to his cheek, as if in thought, and then looked down and announced:

"I accept your proposal of marriage, Cora Lapp."

Then he kissed her, and added: "See how easy that was?"

EPILOGUE

Mary Stoltzfus licked a stamp and affixed it carefully to a big brown envelope. Her mother saw her do it, and murmured:

"Mailing something, Mary?"

Mary looked up at her mother. "I'm entering an essay contest," she told her. "It's a first prize trip to Paris, so why not?"

"Mmm. I see your trip to New York has given you ideas," Fannie Stoltzfus smiled.

Mary looked down at her feet, and answered softly: "I wouldn't have had the nerve to do it three months ago. But after Cora Lapp took me to New York, it was like – I don't know. It was like I woke up."

She looked ruefully at her mother. "When you first brought her to the school, I was mad at you. I thought you were punishing me, or something. But honestly – it's been one of the best things that's ever happened to me."

Her mother reached out and put a gentle hand on her cheek. "Oh, Mary," she sighed, "did you think I did it for Cora? Well, partly. But mostly I did it for you, dear. I *knew* that Cora Lapp would draw you out.

"She does that for *everybody*."

***

It was a drowsy midsummer evening, and Cora sat in Joes' porch swing, pushing off slowly and lazily with one bare foot. Her head was pillowed on Isaac's chest, and his arm was around her.

Katie was sitting in a chair nearby, knitting a little blanket out of soft white yarn, and Joes was inside, laughing and playing with Caleb.

Cora's eye lighted on Katie's knitting, and she asked teasingly: "Have you and Joes decided on a name, Katie?"

Katie pursed her lips. "If it's a boy, we like the name Aaron," she smiled. "And if it's a girl, we're going to call her *Dorathea*."

Cora gasped and looked at her sharply, and Isaac said, "I didn't know you had any relatives with that name."

Katie shook her head. "We don't. But it's a pretty name. We like it."

Cora remembered her beautiful dream, of Katie lifting a baby daughter out of a basket, and the name they had called her – *Dorathea.*

She smiled a bit, and shook her head. Oh Lord, she prayed, I hope that was You just now. Because oh, how lovely if the other surprise in my dream comes true!

She looked up at Isaac, and squeezed his hand, and went back to what she had been doing – listening to the strong, steady beat of his heart beneath her ear.

The End.

LANCASTER COUNTY SECOND CHANCES 4

As Cora and Isaac prepare for their wedding, Katie and Joseph for their baby, and Mary for her trip to Paris, simple mistakes have heart wrenching consequences. How will Katie and Joseph navigate the birth of their first child? Has Cora really accepted her Amish life, or will temptation and Cora's temper force the loss of all she's trying to build? Will Isaac's money troubles lead him to destroy his new marriage? And will Mary's trip to Paris spell herald the beginning of the end of her life with the Amish?

Find out in Lancaster County Second Chances 4.

Chapter One

Isaac Muller sat at the head of the Lapp family dinner table in splendid solitude. He was almost too big for the chair he sat in. Both of his massive elbows were propped on the table, his chin was planted on his fist, and his round blue eyes were on the kitchen door.

Just through that doorway, Cora Lapp pulled a casserole dish from the oven with a pair of cooking mitts. The bubbling concoction trailed a fragrant scent of chicken and cream and mushrooms in the air as she entered the dining room and set it carefully down on the table in front of him.

Isaac leaned over the dish, closed his eyes and inhaled with an expression of pure bliss.

Cora smiled, feeling pleased. Her big blonde fiancé had a farmer's appetite, and was clearly enjoying the table full of dainties she'd prepared for him – all of them his favorites.

It was odd that she loved to watch him enjoy her cooking -- she'd never thought of herself as especially domestic.

But Isaac Muller had a *magical* talent for changing her mind.

Isaac had sneaked up on her. He didn't look a thing like the man she imagined she'd marry one day. He wasn't worldly, he wasn't rich, and he wasn't at all sophisticated. He wanted a traditional Amish wife, and she'd been restless as a wild bird.

Isaac hadn't even been on her radar.

But somehow, now, here she was: she'd come to God, she'd joined the church, she'd promised to obey the *Ordnung*, and was probably going to stay in the county for the rest of her life.

Because of Isaac.

Cora smiled and shook her head. *Who would've thought?*

***

They were alone in her parent's big house. It was Sunday, and after a lifetime of being dragged to worship it felt a little odd to Cora to still be home on a Sabbath. But this was a special day. As was tradition, she and Isaac were enjoying a private meal at home while their engagement was being announced to the community.

Cora bustled back and forth from the kitchen, laden with plates: Isaac's chicken and creamed mushroom sauce, smoked ham with brown sugar glaze, mushrooms in butter, a huge chef salad with boiled eggs and black olives and pine nuts, sweet potato casserole, new peas with tiny pearl onions, crisp little fried apple pies slathered in cream cheese icing, buttery pound cake, and sawdust pie.

Cora piled the plates and dishes around Isaac, taking away the empty ones, and pushing the new ones toward him. She lifted a jug of tea and filled his near-empty glass.

She had been up before dawn that morning, preparing this bountiful meal, and the look of bliss on Isaac's face made it more than worthwhile to her. She was savoring the happiness in his eyes even more than he was enjoying her food.

He looked up at her then, and smiled with his cheeks full

and his lips closed, like a child.

She giggled and dabbed at his chin with a napkin. "Oh, Isaac, you're worse than Caleb!"

When she leaned close, she couldn't resist giving him a kiss. The taste of apples was still on his lips, and to Cora, it was a perfect metaphor – how sweet and simple and *good* Isaac was.

He smelled faintly of the outdoors, of fresh laundry and grass and warm skin, and suddenly she was hungry, *too.*

She slid down into his lap and twined her arms around his neck, curling her fingers in his shining blonde hair. For the first time, she kissed him without any reservation, without worrying, without anything but joy. How she loved the taste of his skin, its subtle salt-sweetness, the firmness of his neck, that strong jaw.

She let her hands wander over his muscular back, along his shoulders, down his arms. How strong and solid he was, and how safe she felt in his arms!

Isaac dropped his knife and fork and folded her in his arms. His hands twined in her hair, softly pulling their silken cords.

That strong, steady heartbeat that she loved was palpable through his shirt now.

Cora's fingers moved to his collar, fretting the topmost

button, but his hands moved to clasp hers. He shook his head.

"No, Cora," he murmured. "Let's wait. We've held out this long. I don't want to do this in your parents' home. I want it to be special. At the cottage."

Cora sighed, listening to the thrumming of her own heartbeat, and rested her brow forlornly against Isaac's. But as much as she hated to admit it, he was right. She wanted that, too.

It was just so hard to behave when Isaac was *so* adorable.

She nodded, and he helped her to stand. She shook out her skirt, and tossed her head, and looked at him with such an expression of irritation that he couldn't help laughing. "Don't worry, Cora," he sputtered. "I promise!"

"You'd better," she warned him, and sat down in the chair beside him.

"See, I have a peace offering for you," he told her. He leaned over, pulled out a mysterious box from underneath his chair, and placed it on the table in front of her...

***

Thank you for Reading!

I hope you enjoyed reading this as much as I loved writing it!

If so, look for Lancaster County Second Chances 4 online in ebook or paperback format.

All the Best,

Ruth Price

ABOUT THE AUTHOR

Ruth Price is a Pennsylvania native and devoted mother of four. After her youngest set off for college, she decided it was time to pursue her childhood dream to become a fiction writer. Drawing inspiration from her faith, her husband and love of her life Harold, and deep interest in Amish culture that stemmed from a childhood summer spent with her family on a Lancaster farm, Ruth began to pen the stories that had always jabbered away in her mind. Ruth believes that art at its best channels a higher good, and while she doesn't always reach that ideal, she hopes that her readers are entertained and inspired by her stories.

54906541R00121

Made in the USA
Lexington, KY
01 September 2016